The Entangled Heart

THE ENTANGLED HEART

Jacqueline Cathcart

AVALON BOOKS
THOMAS BOUREGY AND COMPANY, INC.
401 LAFAYETTE STREET
NEW YORK, NEW YORK 10002

PRINTED IN THE UNITED STATES OF AMERICA
BY HADDON CRAFTSMEN, SCRANTON, PENNSYLVANIA

The Entangled Heart

CHAPTER ONE

To Laurel Miller jogging was a chore, a necessary chore that she performed in the interest of good health, while wondering what masochistic tendency made her continue. If she could only get her mind off the heat, her next breath, and her sluggish, lead-weighted feet, she might be able to mull over this week's happenings.

One week ago she had been hired for a seasonal position by Bellini Brothers Winery, one of the most respected family-owned wine operations in California, and she was now living on the estate. Her position as oenologist was the fulfillment of an academic pursuit. Assistant wine maker. The title felt comfortable; she had earned it.

Behind her, a familiar pattering in the loose gravel of the country surface startled her. *Not again,* she thought. A quick glance revealed the same shaggy, matted beige bundle that might pass for "dog" if scrutinized. This fugitive from some animal shelter seemed to lie in wait for Laurel's everyday workout, ending up on her doorstep to beg. His emaciated appearance and expectant tail wag indicated that he had Laurel pegged as a soft touch, and she hadn't disappointed him.

Laurel hadn't quite succumbed to an adoption, reluctant to approach her new employers with a request so soon after being hired. But it was obvious the dog had no home, and Laurel was already quite taken with him. Behind his scruffy appearance was an indomitable spirit—or at least that's the way she interpreted his persistence. Laurel knew she was a romantic, but she knew also that the moocher—"Mooch" as she already referred to him—had adopted her. It was only a matter of time before she reciprocated, and she hoped Bellini Brothers wouldn't object to the intrusion of a small dog on their property.

Anthony Bellini seemed like a good sort, especially as he had interviewed and hired her. But something about Anthony's reference to his older brother made Laurel keenly aware that the true test in keeping her job was to please Vittorio Bellini.

Laurel had sensed some sort of tension when Tony, as he liked to be called, had described the master of the House of Bellini. He'd seemed guarded but respectful.

"He's not the least like I am," Tony had explained. "He carries the responsibility of the family. You'll meet him soon."

And now this evening the "soon" had come. Vittorio was back from a business trip, and she would meet him—dinner at the House of Bellini. Laurel's excitement was mixed with apprehension.

Continuing down the road, she kept her head bowed to prevent the sun from reaching her already flushed cheeks. Even the tennis visor tucked over her blond ponytail couldn't prevent the sun from toasting her sensitive skin. *I'll be a sight,* she thought. Having what her mother referred to as a "peaches and cream" complexion wasn't always an asset, but there were only a few hundred yards to go to complete the three-mile loop that she had charted so carefully in her Volkswagen that first night.

Intent now, on the last lap, like a horse going to the feed barn, Laurel picked up her pace, only to have her ankle turn in a small chuckhole. She winced, and the sudden hesitation created an entanglement with the small dog, who seemed to get wrapped up in her stride, throwing her off balance onto the road. A skinned knee for that night's important engagement was not in Laurel's plans. She tried to pick herself up, but Mooch insisted on bouncing and licking her face intermittently.

Finally, on all fours, Laurel raised her head slightly, only to see through a somewhat blurred and disoriented perspective a pair of bare masculine legs.

Even at that nose distance away, Laurel was appreciative of the muscular strength that was obvious under the coating of coarse black hair. While contemplating exactly how to gracefully greet this unknown male, she felt herself being hoisted up, suspended in midair, neither foot in touch with the ground. She stared into two large almond-shaped, dark-brown eyes that seemed filled with annoyance.

As he set her down, her gaze passed from arresting eyes to sweat-glistening chest, so close—too close, she thought, aware even in the midst of her embarrassment of a virile presence. He had no sooner placed her on the ground than he stepped back and seemed to inspect her, starting with her toes and working upward.

"You realize you're trespassing?" His low voice seemed to attack her.

"No," she counterattacked. "I work here. I run after work." She stood her ground.

"Oh?" His tone implied doubt.

"I've been here only a week, and thank you for helping me." She tried to appear dignified. "I'm—"

He interrupted, "Do you often make a practice of getting tangled in your dog? That *is* a dog?" His eyes seemed to be amused now. "Is he a running rescue dog, sort of a runner's Saint Bernard?" he continued.

"More of a mugger mutt." She laughed and paused to examine this bronzed, olive-skinned figure of a man blocking her path. He wore nothing but a pair of Levi cutoffs and a pair of running shoes. From her five-foot-four perspective he was easily over six feet tall, but the wide set of his shoulders gave him the appearance of being sturdy—powerful—and his hair was brown like his eyes, so brown as to be almost black.

Sweat dampened his brow. As disordered as Laurel felt, he remained the picture of assurance—certainly not a man who ever fell down or was embarrassed. A hint of determination was there in the set of his jaw and the way he carried his head, straight and erect. Something about him disturbed her, and she stepped forward and to one side to try to get by him. He seemed to sidestep with her, still preventing her exit, while Mooch had gone bananas, yapping and running in circles around the two figures.

"You must be Laurel Miller," he stated.

"Yes." She was startled by the recognition.

"Excuse me." His apology appeared genuine. "I'd momentarily forgotten about our new oenologist. I'm Vittorio Bellini. I just wasn't expecting to meet you this way."

Laurel certainly hadn't expected to meet him that way, either. It was certainly not the preferred way to meet one's new employer. She attempted to look composed but felt somewhat at a disadvantage.

He stepped back and seemed to be categorizing her, much as one would a new wine, she thought—dry, too dry, sweet, too sweet. "I'll see you at dinner tonight?" It was more a statement than a question.

She hoped she had passed as the perfect blend, she thought wryly and met his challenging stare. "I'm looking forward to it."

"Good." He repeated, "Good," and with no further remarks started to run, not a slow jogging pace, but almost a sprint down the path and out of sight.

Laurel watched him disappear in a curve of the road with a reluctant feeling that she'd literally like to run into him again.

Shrugging her shoulders, she walked the rest of the way to her bungalow, thinking about how attractive Vittorio Bellini was. Clearly he looked as if he belonged there. From his even tan, he looked more like a vineyardist than the senior proprietor of the five-hundred-acre Bellini Brothers' winery. But perhaps in such a family-owned operation everyone got involved with the pruning, tying, cultivating, spraying—the all-year-round tasks that insured an abundant and seasoned crop.

Laurel often wondered if she had picked her interest in oenology more for the atmosphere she hoped to live in, than her interests in chemistry and microbiology, which had eventually led her there. Both, she thought, for science had always been a primary interest. She felt comfortable in a discipline where she could move with order, caution, and reason toward a solution.

She stepped onto the small porch of her redwood-framed cottage and looked out at the scene. It was the end of August now, waiting time for the harvest, the leaves dark green, the grapes flushed with color. Row upon row, the vines created a rich tapestry against the earth, and the softness of the hills at sunset seemed a fitting backdrop to the gentle, rolling landscape.

She turned on the light in her small cottage, her new home—two rooms, a bedroom and combination living room and kitchen, with a wood-burning stove. Tony had apologized for the cottage when he'd showed it to her, explaining she was free to live in town, and had seemed surprised at her delight. It was clean, comfortable, and adequate.

Already Laurel's few possessions had added the needed accents necessary to transform house into home. Through the years she had gradually acquired a few furnishings— plump pillows in blue and yellow chintz, a copper teakettle that looked at home on the old stove, and her pride, a small round oak table. Its warm wood tones completed the mood, creating a hospitable atmosphere.

A yip at the front door and the sound of a tail pounding on her wooden porch reminded Laurel that Mooch was not to be forgotten. She put out his usual bowl of nibbles and thought that maybe a bath would make Mooch seem more acceptable as a permanent resident at Bellini Brothers.

The small Swiss clock on the mantel tinged the hour. Only one hour to get ready for her dinner at the big house. Laurel shed her visor, running shorts, and T-shirt, and yanked the rubber band from her ponytail. She turned on the shower, waiting for it to heat, and brushed her shoulder-length hair, thinking about wearing her highest heels in an effort to look more formidable to her new employers. Laurel's friends liked to tease her about her youthful appearance. She supposed someday that would be an advantage, but at twenty-three it sometimes involved explanations that were frankly a nuisance. Perhaps that was why Vittorio Bellini hadn't surmised who she was.

Even so, he had come on a bit strong, but he was a man whose nature generated authority. Nothing had transpired between them but the amenities, and yet the exchange was memorable. True, one didn't fall in a heap at her employer's feet every day, especially on first meeting, and the fact that he just happened to be a handsome man— well, maybe "memorable" wasn't just the right word, and she blushed at her recollections.

Tonight she would make sure that she appeared professional, so she chose a soft green shirtmaker dress to enhance her green eyes.

She rejected the high heels for a pair of plain pumps. After blow-drying her hair and putting on a light makeup, Laurel looked at the whole package. Facing her in the mirror was her petite self, hardly formidable, but all she had to offer the Bellinis.

From her porch she could glimpse the house on the hill. The windows reflected light now, and Laurel took a deep breath, remembering her father's words of advice, which had helped her through so many moments in her life. "All you can do is give it your best," and that's what Laurel had vowed to do on coming here—to give her quality best.

She walked up the long drive. Eucalyptus and poplar cast eerie shadows on the gray stone that dated back to the turn of the century. Since arriving, she had been searching for the right word to describe the Bellini stronghold. *Chateau,* she thought, *a stone chateau*. The stone gave it an appearance of a fortress, but the lines of the arches across the front were softened by horizontal wooden beams on which were carved vines heavy with grapes and the word *Bellini*.

The right wing front on the ground floor was open to the public for wine tasting on weekends and by appointment on weekdays. It was a marvel of masonry, each stone placed to produce a circular room gigantic in size, with windows and doors that opened on to a stone terrace with a view of the vineyards.

The private quarters of the Bellini family,

now just the two brothers, were to the left of the entry and included an entire second floor which encompassed the whole length and width of the building; swimming pool and tennis courts were concealed behind the massive structure.

At the top of the steps a sign read, *Pull for entry.* Laurel gave the woven ropelike sash a tug. A miniature church bell tolled, and the large oak doors opened for her entrance.

Tony greeted her and took her arm in his as if to reassure her, escorting her into a large room where Vittorio Bellini, seated in a red leather armchair, placed a book he was reading on the table beside him, turned, and looked up. A wry smile crossed his face, and he rose to greet her. Laurel gazed, transfixed by the dark, almond-shaped eyes that seemed to hold her in a paralysis.

Tony looked from one to the other. "You know each other?"

"Well, not exactly." Vittorio crossed in front of Tony and held out his hand to Laurel. "We met jogging this afternoon."

Laurel didn't understand why she was reluctant to remove her hand from his clasp.

Seeing him again only further emphasized that Vittorio Bellini was not what she had expected at all. True, he was different from Tony, who was tall, lean, and aquiline, and closer to her own age. But Tony had made Vittorio sound so old and stuffy. He was older, but only somewhere in his mid-thirties, and in his jogging shorts—well, "old and stuffy" were hardly the words.

"Hello," she managed. "Thank you again for helping me this afternoon."

"I'm sorry I didn't recognize who you might be, but in your running outfit...." He smiled. "You looked"—he hesitated—"different, and then, too, there was your interesting dog."

Tony looked startled. "A dog?"

"Yes, Miss Miller has a very entertaining dog."

Laurel didn't think Vittorio's remark all that humorous. Even considering Mooch, he was overdoing it a little. She looked at Tony and tried to explain. "Well, he's not exactly my dog. Mooch just sort of adopted me, and I was going to ask if I could keep him."

"Mooch?" Vittorio threw his head back and laughed out loud. It was a deep, musical sound that filled the room, and it was infectious. "Well, it's settled then. With a name like Mooch, we can hardly turn him away, but see that he doesn't get tangled in the vines or your feet," Vittorio added.

Tony went to a corner of the room, and on a small table were some glass decanters. "Some sherry to toast Laurel and Mooch."

And, lifting their glasses, the three of them joined in the toast. "To Laurel." Vittorio focused his eyes on her. "And Mooch," he repeated.

Adjoining the comfortable living room was a small, intimate dining room with the table set for four. Rust and yellow chrysanthemums in a clear crystal bowl graced the chocolate-brown linen cloth. In the candlelight the room took on an old-world appearance. Bustling about the table, filling the water glasses, was a woman in a soft rose dress, her figure round but not fat. Her hair was streaked with gray and tied in a tidy bun at the nape of her neck. She glanced at the three of them.

"Dinner in five minutes." It was not stated in a dictatorial manner, but one had the impression of authority and that the assemblage had better be ready.

"Angie," Vittorio called, "please come and meet our new oenologist, Laurel. Without Angie," he explained, "we would all be very thin and undernourished."

Angie's face seemed to light at the praise. "It's about time we had another woman around here." She stepped toward Laurel and gave her a kiss on both cheeks.

Laurel was surprised, but she responded to the warmth of Angie's greeting with a blush and a squeeze of her hand. "I'm glad to be here too." Angie smiled and headed for the kitchen.

"Angie was with us even before the accident," Vittorio commented. He hesitated. "You know?"

"I know, and I'm very sorry." Yes, Laurel and everyone in wine circles knew of Vittorio, senior, and Maria Bellini's untimely deaths in an airplane crash less than a year ago. Laurel remembered how she had felt when her father had died of a heart attack several years ago, but to lose both your parents at once. . . . She felt inadequate with her reply.

Sitting down at the table, Vittorio went on, "You understand our parents have left us an important legacy here. Their sound investments have provided the means for us to continue the winery, but times are getting more difficult. Every day foreign and corporate investors are buying more of California's wine interests. Family-owned operations, like ours, that care about wine quality even more than profit are in a fragile position."

Laurel sympathized with his viewpoint. She hated to see the family-owned wineries displaced.

"We must become more competitive without losing our integrity," he continued. "At Christmas, for example, we will introduce a new white wine to meet the market's demands."

"But," Tony interrupted, "you must admit, Vittorio, that because of these large interests, more Americans are aware of wine, and all wineries stand to gain from their awareness."

"As far as I'm concerned, they're not welcome." Vittorio's face hardened, and his dark eyes flashed a warning. The subject had been closed.

Dinner was delicious—a shrimp cocktail with a white wine, a broth, and a pasta dish that Laurel had never tasted before.

Vittorio turned to Laurel. "I'm surprised that you were attracted to our ad, Laurel, that you didn't seek one of the larger operations. Our ranch seems like an isolated atmosphere for a young woman."

Vittorio's remarks were said in a tone that seemed to question Laurel's status, as if she didn't know what she had been doing coming here. Reaching this goal had taken her a while, what with working and school combined, but she had done it without leaning on anyone. The winery was a peaceful atmosphere to reflect in after what seemed a long struggle. What gave him the right to challenge her decision?

"I considered other alternatives," she replied, "but I respect quality too. Your house has a fine reputation, and I feel very fortunate to be here to work under your winemaker, Emidio Izzo. I'm a quiet sort of person, used to making my own amusements."

"Is your family in the area?" Vittorio continued to probe.

"My mother and stepfather are in Minnesota, and my brother and his family in Vermont." It was still difficult for Laurel to think of Walter as a substitute father. She was happy for her mother to start a new life. She was fond of Walter, but he entered her own life too late. She had deliberately chosen to remain in California, and because of her profession it was the best place to be.

She added, "Air travel makes distances closer."

"I hope you won't get bored with us."

"Come on now, Vittorio," Tony interceded. "Let's be just glad she chose to stay. What a welcome, to question her sanity!"

"Not her sanity, Tony. Her credentials were outstanding. I just want to be certain that Laurel understands what she's getting into here as the only female in our employ."

"Until now, no one has concerned themselves with my sex." The words just seemed to blurt out of Laurel.

"That seems impossible," Vittorio responded quickly.

Laurel was surprised at her outburst and annoyed with his reply. It was hardly the thing to say when she wanted so to make a good impression. Vittorio seemed to be looking at her with admiration, which only increased her discomfort, and she was thankful that Angie chose that moment to serve a fruit compote. She concentrated on eating her dessert, conscious of Vittorio's studied expression. He constantly seemed to be measuring her.

After dinner Tony offered to walk her to her cottage. Laurel glanced at Vittorio. His face registered a brief scowl, and it was plain to Laurel that he didn't want his precious brother to perform such an act, to be contaminated by this female employee, who wouldn't be good enough for a Bellini heir, she sensed. Although she liked Tony, she, too, didn't want it to go any further. She could handle her work better without emotional complications.

"Thank you, Tony, but that won't be necessary. It's only a short distance."

"I'll watch you from the drive," he insisted.

Laurel graciously accepted and turned to Vittorio, extending her hand. "Thank you for a lovely evening."

"It's our custom to welcome a new employee." His hand barely touched hers.

An employee! Yes, he was making it quite plain—that was her role here. Her college classes had prepared her well for this job, but this opportunity to work at one of the finest wineries in California was the answer to a dream. She must not forget her place.

The light Laurel had left on in her front window welcomed her, and she waved to Tony from the drive, indicating her safe arrival. A throaty growl startled her, but growl turned into greeting, and Mooch bounced out of the darkness with a more than enthusiastic welcome.

"How long have you been here, fellow?" Laurel patted his side and stroked his head. "You've been approved, Mooch, by the boss himself."

Laurel was confused. She was not at all

certain that *she* had secured Vittorio Bellini's approval. The entire evening she felt as if she had been on trial, and she didn't know what verdict had been reached. Vittorio's attitudes seemed to go back and forth between charming and borderline rudeness. Instinct told her that her femininity bothered him, and her feelings for him were a mixed bag. She was drawn to him, yet alienated by his authority. She tried to push aside the feelings that surged through her every time Vittorio's eyes had met hers, and reminded herself she had only to prove herself by doing a good job.

CHAPTER TWO

The next morning over a cup of coffee, Laurel reflected on her first days at the winery. Emidio Izzo was a superb mentor. She wished that the tentative contract date read beyond January, that she could study under him for several years. For the making of wine was more than test-tube chemistry. It required having a memory bank of wines gained from experience, and Emidio had this —a memory and skill of perceiving that Laurel knew would take her years to develop even with her extensive scientific background.

She had been hired to help with the crush and the weeks that followed. Tony had been vague as to when and whether it was contingent on her performance or Vittorio's assessment of her capabilities.

At any rate, she and Emidio had hit it off. He was patient and kind. The things she had learned in school and summer work-study were beginning to jell with actuality.

She rinsed the coffee cup, pulled on a wool sweater, and carried her jacket, heading toward the lab. No matter how early she seemed to be, Emidio was earlier, his gray head now visible in the window. He smiled when she entered, pointing to the stack of paperwork on his desk, shaking his head.

"If the government gives me one more form to fill out, I'll have to fill the wine bottles with vintage scrap paper. Did you see the color?" There was no pause between the sentences.

"The color?" she questioned.

"The grapes! You should always be looking at the grapes." He grasped her hand and pulled her toward the door. "Good grapes make good wine." The sun glanced off the fields. Already, weeding was completed, each row neat and tidy. They trudged up the hill a distance from the lab, examining the grapes on the slope.

"These will be ready first," Emidio explained. "See the color, the size. We'll begin measuring the sugar content more often now and determine when to pick."

Laurel appreciated the reference "we."

"And now to work." And with the same enthusiasm and vigor that marked their uphill climb, Emidio pulled her down the hill, and they entered the cellars together. Laurel slipped on her jacket.

"Even on the hottest days, our cellars remain a constant fifty to fifty-five degrees," Emidio explained.

Others were busy working on hoppers, conveyers, hoists, pumps, and fermentation vats, checking and cleaning equipment with a sense of expectancy in the atmosphere.

The cellars' stone walls engulfed them, three to twelve feet thick in places, cut into the hillside, a perfect environment for making wine.

In the binning shelters, the wine was being bottled in order to make room for the approaching harvest. Laurel spent the rest of the day testing the bottling, putting samples in the wine library for future reference. The lab was little more than an antiseptic kitchen. The stainless-steel sinks, white counter tops, beakers, and funnels were hers to keep clean. Although the pace was somewhat relaxed now, Emidio had warned her to store up her energy; when the harvest was in full swing, their work schedule would be into the night.

She washed the last thermometer and was about to place it in its assigned place when the door suddenly opened. Vittorio entered and glanced in her direction, and the slippery tube dropped between her fingers to the floor, glass and mercury scattering in all directions.

"I didn't mean to startle you." Vittorio

looked nonchalant, as if she hadn't dropped forty-five dollars on the floor.

Her first instinct was to bend down and pick up the fragments, but she felt his hand on her elbow, restraining her.

"No," he cautioned. "The mercury, to say nothing of cutting yourself."

She stood up, conscious of his authoritative presence now close beside her, which for some reason added to her predicament. She quickly went and got the broom and dustpan. Vittorio made no further comment and leaned against the counter, sipping a cup of coffee that he poured from the ongoing pot. He just stood there, observing her.

Laurel felt her face flush. *It's the way he looks at me, or is it just my imagination?* Every time she was with him, she seemed more aware of her femininity, and certainly more aware of his masculinity, which did little to help her equilibrium. She bent over to scoop up the mess.

"Emidio?" Vittorio asked, seemingly oblivious to her discomfort.

"He's in the cellars."

"The forecast is for hot weather the next few days."

"We've stepped up the testing of the grapes."

"Ask him to check the vines near the house, the new hybrid. We've been developing the stock for seven years now."

"A new grape?" Laurel's voice revealed her excitement.

"It *is* exciting." He seemed pleased with her response. "I hope you'll enjoy your work with us. Emidio says good things already about your performance."

"Thank you. Emidio is a master teacher," she replied, but her mind was racing with other thoughts. *Does he realize how he's looking at me? Is this his way of apologizing for last night's rudeness? I don't need this or want this. Need or want what?* Her mind was definitely playing tricks with her, and she wished he'd leave.

"Have a nice weekend, Laurel." He closed the door quietly behind him.

She finished up her last task, scribbled a brief note to Emidio, reporting her conversation with Vittorio and her catastrophe with the thermometer, locked the door of the lab, and saw a familiar shape bound up the road to greet her.

"Down, down!" she shouted at Mooch, who seemed to spring the length of her whole body in an effort to lick her face. In defeat, she bent and petted the wiggling bit of fluff, and he soon calmed down enough to follow at her heels toward the cottage.

"I missed you this morning," she told Mooch.

His tail responded with the precision of a metronome, and he bounded up the steps, looking expectantly at the door.

"This is off limits," Laurel said, scooting in the door, "at least until you've had a bath."

Mooch settled on the porch, resigned to his position until she brought out a bowl of food, which he promptly attacked.

It was twilight now, but still time for Laurel's evening jog, and she started up the hill behind the chateau, past the lab, and up the road access to the fields. As she passed the house, she noticed a sleek, red Ferrari parked in the drive. It started with a smooth, effortless howl, the engine noise intruding on the landscape, and roared down the drive at a fast clip.

Laurel watched the car careen down the drive and almost attack the highway below. Her picture of Vittorio changed with every encounter. His love of family, the land, the wine—and now blondes and fast cars. She supposed that it wasn't unusual for a man of his means to own a Ferrari, but she had pictured him more the Mercedes type. *Well, first impressions are often not valid,* she thought, slowing her pace up a steeper incline, Mooch now at her heels once again.

Alone at the top of the hill, she turned to survey the countryside below. The lights of the main house were visible, the one wing a cylindrical beacon, the vines to her left and right thick, rigid columns which had lost their identifiable quality in the dusk. She sat on a log by the side of the road, grateful for Mooch's company.

Laurel had a feeling of déjà-vu. She had been here before in her imagination, and beside her in the fantasy was someone holding her hand. At one time she thought it might be Rick, but that was over now. After the abrupt death of her father, she hadn't been able to extend her emotions. For a time she had transferred her feelings of dependency and need to Rick, and she thought she had loved him. But the year before she graduated, Rick's love for her had vanished when he got his diploma. At first she was crushed, but now she was glad it was finished. The only thing they had in common was that they went to the same school, and their bond had been comfortable but not exciting.

All of a sudden the serenity of the moment turned to an overwhelming feeling of loneliness. She swallowed and fought against what seemed an irrational emotion. She was where she wanted to be, doing what she had chosen to do, but the tears won out, sliding onto her cheeks, and she wondered at her vulnerability. She stood, took a deep breath, and walked purposefully back down the route she had traveled, determined to fill the remaining hours of this Friday evening with something besides reasonless self-pity.

She showered, changed into a pair of nice slacks and a light sweater, and backed out of her driveway, aware that Mooch's down-tail posture expressed his sentiments at being left behind. Her Volkswagen sounded little

more than a large lawn mower in contrast to
the roar of Vittorio's Ferrari, the sound still
lingering in the back of her mind. The small,
worn car had been a faithful old friend,
always taking her where she wanted to go.
She pulled onto the highway and headed the
five miles to town.

The town seemed remote from its sister
cities that had grown into acres of tract hous-
ing, shopping malls, and the resultant free-
way access that accompanied them.

Small-town California was still here, and
part of its protection was its location, north of
San Francisco, in a small valley with its
vineyards, so far at least, holding their own
against the greed of land developers.

Laurel parked on the town square, a small
park, and walked the perimeter past antique
shops and galleries, closed now for the day.
The lights of the pharmacy looked inviting,
and she went inside, delighted to find an old-
fashioned soda fountain open for business.

She ordered a banana split, and when the
young man behind the counter brought her
the three scoops, outlined with banana,
crested with three sauces, nuts, and whipped
cream, she thought that there was nothing
like such sinful indulgence to chase the blues
away. She sat at the small, round ice-cream
table, concentrating on preventing the con-
coction from teetering all over the table as
each spoonful undermined its delicate balance.

"Are you sure you can finish that?" a familiar voice asked.

Laurel looked up to see Tony enter the pharmacy. She smiled. "I'm not at all sure. Want to help out?"

Tony sat down and ordered a soda. "This is a surprise. I was looking for you earlier, but all I could find was Mooch, who, incidently, guards your door as if he were a Doberman."

Laurel laughed at the comparison. "I just thought I'd come to town and see what's happening on a Friday night."

"Well, if it's high-powered entertainment you're after, this is it," and he waved his hand at the pharmacy.

"Never had a better banana split," she said.

"I thought you might like to try a movie. They specialize in old films, but some of them are good."

Laurel hesitated. She had made up her mind to keep her private life separate from that of the Bellinis', but then this wasn't a date, and she would make that clear to Tony.

"I'd like that, Tony. What's playing?"

"Let's put it this way—it's the only show in town."

Laurel managed to finish the last bite, and Tony looked at her with awe. "I really didn't think you'd be able to do that."

"Practice, practice." She laughed. "I'll justify it with jogging an extra mile tomorrow."

Out on the street, Tony pointed to a vintage marquee. "Show's over there." They crossed the square to the theater.

"I thought towns like this didn't exist anymore," Laurel said.

"They're at a premium, but I'm a city boy at heart. My idea of living would be to have an apartment overlooking the Golden Gate. In fact, if it wasn't for Vittorio's needing me right now, I'd be off and running. I'm an attorney."

"You are?" Laurel was surprised.

"I had just passed the bar when my parents..." Tony's voice trailed. "Well, I'm needed here now. I'm biding my time."

"Does Vittorio know how you feel?"

"There hasn't been the opportunity, and he's so wrapped up in the winery that— Oh, well, one of these days. Don't mention this to him, Laurel. It would only make him feel he's keeping me against my will, and for now it isn't that way. I'll tell him when the time is right. Vittorio would have a hard time understanding why anyone would want to leave the ranch. He belongs there, with the land and the wine."

In front of the box office, Tony reached into his back pocket for his wallet, and simultaneously Laurel thrust her money in his hand.

"Nothing doing," he protested.

She was firm. "This is the only way I'll go, Tony. Believe me, it's—"

"Are you trying to tell me something?"

"It's just that I'm an employee, and I just feel—"

"No mix, you mean, business and pleasure." He smiled. "Okay, Laurel, whatever makes you feel comfortable."

Laurel hadn't even looked at what was playing, but it was an old film she hadn't seen before. It was about auto racing and had many exciting scenes of skill and danger. She found it hard to identify with why anyone would risk his life in such a profession. When one of the cars hit the wall and exploded into flames, she buried her head against Tony's arm.

"I wonder if Vitto knows about this flick," Tony commented as they strolled out of the theater. "This is just his cup of tea. The only inconsistency of my older brother is that his love of automobiles almost challenges his love of winemaking. Behind the wheel of his Ferrari, he becomes a madman."

"Now, Tony, don't you think that's a bit of an exaggeration?" Vittorio said, having come up behind them. Once again he seemed to concentrate on Laurel.

The lobby of the small theater was filled with his presence, and Laurel observed the striking blonde beside him who was seemingly sewn to his sleeve.

"You must be the cute little thing that Vitto has told me about," the blonde said. The words were poured out like sweet syrup.

"Pamela," Vittorio intervened, "this is Laurel, our new oenologist at the ranch."

"You seem so young to be out of school." Again her voice was sweet but venomous. "Vitto, isn't it amazing? I swear, she looks so young." Pamela's remarks seemed to negate Laurel's presence. It was as if she weren't there, a flesh-and-blood person, just some object to be discussed.

It was instant dislike on both their parts, but Laurel had to concede that Pamela was gorgeous. She hung on to Vittorio's arm as if Laurel were a predator. *If she only knew,* Laurel thought, *she could relax.* But maybe when a woman went with a man as attractive as Vittorio, she had to worry about that.

Tony stepped forward. "And what have you been doing with yourself lately, Pam? I haven't seen you around for a while."

"I just got back from a buying trip in the East. I was telling Vittorio that he must come to the gallery soon, and you, too, Tony. I'm sure you'll love the latest collection. I've been trying to convince him to show art on the walls of the wine-reception room."

"We're a winery, Pamela, not a gallery." Vittorio's firm statement ended the discussion. He looked for a moment at Laurel and Tony. "I didn't think racing pictures were your interest, Tony."

"Only thing in town."

"And how did you like the film?" Vittorio asked, looking at Laurel.

"Frightening but exciting."

Pamela stage-whispered to Vittorio, "We'd better be going, darling. It was nice meeting you, Miss..."

"Laurel is her name," Tony filled in.

Vittorio turned to leave, but not before giving Laurel and Tony a look that seemed to imply disapproval. Laurel felt suddenly chilled, as if a cool breeze had blown over her. She headed with Tony across the square to her car and hesitated.

"I had the impression that your brother wasn't happy to see us together, Tony. I don't want to be the cause of any trouble between you."

"That's crazy! It's none of his business what I do with my time, anyway."

Laurel debated whether to drop the conversation right there, and she wished she hadn't started it. "Maybe he thinks, and rightly so, that an employee and—"

"That's a bit much, Laurel, over a movie, and not even a date at that."

"Well, he's your brother and —"

"My brother, not my keeper."

They sat down on a bench at the edge of the park, and Laurel could see Vittorio and Pamela across the way, walking toward the Ferrari. "She's beautiful." Laurel voiced her thoughts.

"Pamela?" Tony nodded. "Yes, very. I guess that's what Vittorio sees in her. They went to high school together. Pam was a couple of years behind him, a cheerleader. Every boy in town wanted to date her and probably did until Vittorio noticed her. He was a senior, and they were a pair until he graduated. She fancies herself an art dealer, studied abroad. I guess she's not that bad, just spoiled and used to getting what she wants, and right now it's obvious she wants my brother."

"I don't see him resisting," Laurel remarked and wished she hadn't said that, either. What did she care?

"Vittorio is only into the art of making wine." Tony laughed. "He's married to the wine. Wine runs through his veins, red wine. With Vittorio, it's always the ranch first, and in this regard he's an immovable purist. But enough of this. I certainly didn't want to bore you with family matters. I enjoyed your company, Laurel. It's nice to have someone to talk to."

They were at her car now. "Thank you, Tony, for the introduction to town."

It had been a fun evening except for the encounter with Vittorio. His attitude had conveyed a disapproval of her association with Tony, and she regretted that he had read more into the relationship. She wanted her work judged without prejudice.

She was glad to see Mooch's friendly face when she got to the cottage. "At least I've made a big hit with you," she said. Mooch thumped his tail on the porch in response.

Tomorrow she would be busy putting her

house in order. She'd hardly had time since her arrival to organize her kitchen or bedroom. There was grocery shopping, laundry, and a bath for Mooch.

She snuggled under the sheets, tired, and thought how glad she was that she didn't have to get up early. Just as she was about to go to sleep, she heard the throb of an engine —the Ferrari was back. She heard it pulse up the drive, seeming to hesitate for a moment by the cottage, then gun its engine and fade. *This is ridiculous!* she chided herself, but for some reason she felt better—Vittorio was home.

CHAPTER THREE

The struggle to improve Mooch's appearance with a bath was more than Laurel counted on. Mooch, for all his endearing qualities, was not fond of being watered down. Laurel tied him to a large tree, brushed him down, and cut the matted fur. Just as she had him lathered with soap, he twisted loose and dashed underneath the porch steps, out of reach. His pathetic expression of being betrayed might have, under other circumstances, melted Laurel's heart, but at that moment her feelings came closer to rage.

Mooch scrunched in the dirt under the porch, and Laurel, on all fours, tried to entice him out with pleadings, threats, and finally —as a last straw—puppy biscuits. She shook the box. Seeing the prize, Mooch couldn't resist the temptation and timidly inched forward in her direction, an effort to reach the promised treat without sacrificing his safe position. Laurel grabbed for the scruff of his neck and a tug of war ensued that resulted in Mooch's captivity.

"Darn you, Mooch!" Laurel shook him and placed him once more firmly in front of the hose. "Look at you," she went on.

Mooch just put his tail between his legs, and Laurel hosed him down and took some fluffy towels to rub him dry. The minute the towels touched him, Mooch's expression changed to gratitude, and he licked Laurel, his tail wagging once again.

"You're impossible." Laurel was laughing now, unable to be permanently angry with such a friendly opponent.

Her struggle with Mooch had soaked her from her T-shirt and shorts to her tennis shoes. Moisture and suds mixed with gravel and dirt, and in her bent-over position, the tiny rocks bit into her knees. The sun was full, but in spite of its rays she was a bit chilled.

"Who's taking the bath?" She heard Vittorio's voice behind her.

She laughed. "It's a toss-up, but right now Mooch is ahead on the cleanliness score." Laurel wanted to run and hide behind the tree. Standing there with her wet T-shirt clinging to her, she knew she presented a bedraggled picture, certainly not the image of capability that she wanted to be.

"So this is the new Mooch." Vittorio

walked around Mooch and Laurel with an appraising glance. "It's surprising what a bath will do."

"I didn't exactly plan on bathing too," she said with a nervous laugh.

He changed the conversation abruptly. "Did you enjoy your outing in our big town?"

"Yes, very much."

"And the movie?"

"Yes, I was glad I ran into Tony in town and that he suggested it." This was her chance to set the record straight, show him it was just a casual outing.

"My brother is good company," he stated quite formally, as if he were delivering a lecture.

Laurel didn't quite know what to reply. Just what was he trying to get at? "Yes, he is."

"I'm glad he's taken it upon himself to make you feel at home here, Laurel."

The words sounded harmless enough, but the tone in which they were delivered negated the message.

"Are you unhappy he hired me?" Once again Laurel regretted her natural impulse to be candid.

But Vittorio didn't seem surprised by the question. "Not if you can do the work, but I do want you to understand us here. Our business is wine, and I don't want your social life to interfere with your job."

"I can assure you, Mr. Bellini, that will not

be a problem. My job here and the wine are my first considerations." Laurel's gaze was steady as she met his.

"I'm glad we understand each other, Laurel."

"Perfectly," she replied. "And now if you'll excuse me, I must change out of these wet clothes." She turned her back on Vittorio, left him standing beside Mooch, and went into the house.

How dare he! she thought as she flung her wet shirt and shorts across the room. *How dare he presume!* She was still burning with unreleased anger when she stepped into the shower, and it wasn't until she was dry and in clean clothes that she simmered down. Of course, as Tony had said, his brother was married to the wine, but even so, for him to assume in advance that she might be distracted from her job infuriated her.

She finished out the weekend intent on her plan to put her house in order and to push aside her antagonistic feelings toward Vittorio, but the house tasks were more easily accomplished. Every time she saw his red Ferrari pass the cottage, she toyed with the childish notion of at least letting the air out of his tires. One thing, she decided, Vittorio was not a man one could ignore easily, in or out of his Ferrari.

* * *

The weather pattern had changed to un-
seasonably hot, and Laurel was busy every
day measuring the grape sugar. If the hot
weather lasted so close to harvest, there
could be important decisions to be made. Pro-
longed heat at this critical stage could cause
sunburn, the grapes might split, resulting in
juice loss, possible mold, bees—too many
variables, she thought. She was glad that the
ultimate decisions as to when to pick and
when to cool the vineyards belonged to Emidio, and she hoped the heat would quit before
a no-win situation developed.

Simultaneously with her thinking, Emidio
came in from the fields. "If this heat doesn't
quit, we'll be picking them all at once." He
looked concerned. "To think I was wishing for
a little warm weather to up the sugar, but
not this. Pray for less heat, Laurel."

In her student days Laurel had worked in
wineries at harvest time, but this time it was
different. This time she was involved with
the decision making, and the anticipated
harvest was exciting to her. A tension filled
the air, an expectancy, like waiting for the
curtain to go up on opening night at the theater. Something important was about to happen.

She saw Vittorio out in the fields, inspecting the vines, hardly distinguishable from
the fieldhands, his dark head and bare torso

barely visible in the midst of the thick fo-
liage. She could identify with his feelings for
the wine, all this nurturing to produce a
product.

The next morning Laurel awakened to a
light rain. She quickly dressed and rushed to
the lab.

"Heat, now rain." Emidio looked out at the
scene.

Vittorio entered, his words a repetition,
"Heat, now rain. No wonder we have the saying, 'Nothing is certain until one draws the
cord.'" He looked worried. "What's the forecast?"

"Only today," Emidio assured him. "And
we'll start picking day after tomorrow, no
matter what the mud."

Vittorio looked at Laurel. "You're quite
early."

"I was concerned too. Do you think we'll
have mildew?"

"Not if the sun shines tomorrow." Vittorio's
voice was filled with concern. "It's not in our
hands now."

"The sun will shine tomorrow," Laurel
stated emphatically.

"You have some inside information?" Vittorio's hearty laugh relieved the tension.

"No." She smiled. "I just like happy end-
ings."

Vittorio seemed to study her face. "Why
not?" And with this statement the gloom in
the lab office seemed to lift. Hot coffee served

to warm their insides too. At least temporarily, there was a conviviality that wiped out the stormy atmosphere.

Even though the next day was Sunday, Laurel dressed in jeans and a warm sweater and hurried to the winery to help Emidio, thankful that her prophecy for sunshine had materialized.

He held the hydrometer for her to see. "Tomorrow we pick these."

She worked beside him, recording the readings on the various grape samples, and then they went into the cellars. Just outside the doors Vittorio and Tony were working on a crusher, Vittorio's body just visible beneath the big piece of equipment. He came out and said to Tony, "Now try it." The motor reverberated throughout the courtyard. Vittorio looked triumphant and turned to Laurel. "I think we're ready. Thank you for the sunshine and the slight wind is welcome too."

Tony looked puzzled.

"Laurel ordered the weather for us," Vittorio explained. "Being able to order the weather is a rare and special quality in an oenologist—right, Emidio?"

"And she is pretty as well as extremely capable," Emidio said.

"No argument with that," Tony agreed.

Vittorio smiled. "No argument."

Maybe Laurel had finally won over the master of Bellini. Maybe this was his first concession that he had been wrong. Anyway, she would accept that. She wasn't one to hold a grudge.

"We shouldn't give me too much credit," she countered, "especially on Sunday."

"Right you are, Laurel." Vittorio looked thoughtful. "Mama and Papa would be disappointed in us if they could hear us. We must go to church and make amends. Be ready in ten minutes," he told the group.

Tony interceded, "Maybe Laurel would prefer—"

"No, I'd like to go," she interrupted.

Laurel hastily brushed her hair and changed into a cotton print and a light sweater and headed for the main house. Before she had walked up the drive, the Ferrari's throaty motor could be heard coming toward her, and she stepped aside. Vittorio stopped beside her and motioned her to get in.

Beside him on the tan leather seat, she was captured by his profile. Such a strong man, she thought, yet perhaps vulnerable, for there was something in his eyes, something hidden there.

Her thoughts were interrupted by his voice, which said almost in a whisper, "Mama would be pleased with you," and then quickly added, "for getting us to church. We haven't been going since the accident, but somehow today.... I hope I didn't presume on you."

"No, I must admit I haven't been attending

much, either, since I've been out on my own. It's good to be reminded."

"Well, then, good."

The roar of the engine was all that could be heard between them now. Laurel found it hard to believe that she was riding so amiably by Vittorio's side after all that had been said between them in the last few weeks. She was grateful, but not for the way he was driving.

They careened down the highway, taking the curves on what felt like two wheels. She held on to the door tightly, her knuckles white, and she gasped involuntarily, thinking that if they made it to church in one piece, she would have a lot to be thankful for. Looking through the side-view mirror, she could not even see Tony and Emidio in Tony's Porsche.

Vittorio didn't even seem to notice her. The wheel seemed to be an extension of his body. What was it that Tony had said that night at the theater? "He becomes a madman behind the wheel."

On the next curve she controlled her fear no longer and shouted, "Vittorio!"

He turned and looked at her, slowed the engine down and said, "I'm sorry, Laurel. I forget I'm not on the track sometimes."

"You race?" she asked.

"Not often, because of the time, but when I can. I've got a '57 Ferrari, and vintage-car racing is not too demanding."

"I've never been to a race, but the movie version the other night almost put me under my seat."

"It's really quite safe, especially that kind, if you know what you're doing. For me it's a release, a freedom from responsibility. On the track I'm exhilarated. It's hard to explain, but to be able to control a powerful engine, to have her respond to your touch, to gentle her around a curve—" He stopped. "I sound—"

"It sounds like a love affair." Laurel laughed nervously.

"You're probably right. I love making wine; I love fast cars. They're my two passions." He looked thoughtful.

The car stopped. Laurel was unaware that they were already at the church. She could look only at Vittorio. His dark eyes seemed to bore right through her. His passion—that was the quality that held her now. His passions, for making wine, for living wholly, totally, seared her without a touch. She yearned to be in his arms. Nothing had transpired, yet she was trembling under his gaze. She was grateful for the sight of the Porsche now pulling up beside them, and she grabbed for the door handle.

Vittorio's hand closed on her left arm, preventing her from getting out of the car. He forced her with that one movement to turn slightly and look at him once again. Did he realize how she was feeling? He released his hold, came around to her side, avoiding her eyes, and opened the door. She hurried into the sanctity of the church, the men following.

Kneeling, she felt momentarily safe, protected. But even as she prayed for wisdom and sanity, even as the rituals of childhood soothed and stroked her into control, she knew that in spite of herself Vittorio Bellini attracted her as no other man had ever done before, and she was afraid and confused.

Leaving the church building, Laurel kept her distance from Vittorio.

"Want to try a Porsche home?" Tony offered.

She glanced at Vittorio, hesitating. Tony went on, "It's a different kind of ride."

Vittorio went to the Porsche and opened the passenger side, indicating for Laurel to get in. There was no smile on his face. In fact, Laurel couldn't read any emotion there, but it was plain that he agreed with Tony's proposal. Laurel, not knowing what else to do, complied with the direction. The choice had been made for her, and she looked at Tony, who didn't seem to notice the tension she felt.

"Riding with me won't be the racy experience you had getting here, but a Porsche is a good ride, and I promise you'll see the countryside on the route home," Tony said.

Riding back to the winery, Laurel's thoughts were on anything but the landscape. Now, removed from Vittorio's presence, she wondered if she had fabricated her feelings. Had Vittorio noticed? This was not what she had intended to happen. To be attracted to any man, let alone her employer, was not in her plans.

She was glad to be riding back with Tony, to have a chance to regain her composure. If what she had felt was recognized by Vittorio, he gave no indication, and his thrusting her into Tony's car indicated that either way, she was just not that important to him. After all, a man like Vittorio was probably used to females swooning about. Her feelings, even though momentary, were ridiculous. If she were to continue at Bellini Brothers, her contacts with Vittorio would have to be businesslike.

"Laurel, you're not listening to a word I'm saying."

"I'm sorry, Tony. I guess I let my mind wander. I'm enjoying the ride, and I'm glad you aren't a race-car driver."

"Not me. I'm too sane for that."

"Does Vittorio race often?"

"No, just when he gets the chance, and sometimes he just drives the course in the Ferrari for kicks. He's known at the track, has a lot of friends there. I guess that's Vittorio's way of breaking loose, but it's not my way." Tony looked lost in his own thoughts, then returned to the present. "Maybe you wouldn't mind joining me in the city today. I could use the company."

Laurel debated momentarily, remembering Vittorio's lecture, but what she did in her free time was her business, and something about Tony's manner made her feel he needed a friend. A day in San Francisco was just what she needed, too, she rationalized. Being isolated these past few weeks had probably affected her brain.

Tony dropped her off in front of her cottage. "Pick you up in a half hour. Be sure and bring your jacket," he advised. "Never know what the weather is like in the city."

Laurel had just closed the door of the Porsche when she heard the Ferrari roar up and pass them. She jumped back involuntarily, the sound startling her. A fleeting look at the red streak as it moved up the grade made her momentarily reconsider the excursion. She dismissed the thought. She and Tony were just friends, no chemistry there. She hurried to change her clothes and deposited some food and water on the porch for Mooch in case of a late return.

Approaching the city from the Marin side, Laurel was always impressed by its clean look, especially on a day like this one, with the sun full. Laurel loved San Francisco.

The towers of the Golden Gate Bridge reached skyward until they seemed to almost touch the clouds. Tony slowed for the toll booth and veered left down on the Marina.

"This is where I want to live." Tony pointed to the homes that fronted the yacht harbor. "After the harvest I'm going to speak to Vittorio. It's just that sometimes he's so hard to talk to. Selling out to the corporations would be like trampling on Mama's and Papa's graves—I agree with him on that—and we have to become more competitive. I could work on the marketing end from here and practice law too."

Laurel didn't know quite what to say. She didn't need to use her imagination to know that Vittorio was difficult to talk to. He seemed to start and end all their conversations. She could sympathize with Tony and at the same time understand Vittorio's feeling of paternal protection toward the winery. And besides, she reminded herself, *it wasn't her business.*

"I'm sure it will work out for both of you," she commented and changed the subject. Today she wanted to forget the winery, forget Vittorio.

At Ghirardelli Square, sipping coffee-russe topped with gobs of whipped cream in steaming, glass bowl-shaped mugs, Laurel felt contented. Certainly all was right with this world at this particular moment. Laurel basked in these pauses in her life when thought was confined to no more than the pleasant moment at hand.

She and Tony browsed the shops and galleries, and Laurel purchased a poster print of golden poppies that leaped from their slick paper surface. In an adjacent gallery were some outstanding moderns with equally outstanding price tags. She pointed to the four-figure tag on a symphony of color, a water-color wash that was so intense, so pure and fresh that Laurel was spellbound by its beauty.

"You should buy it for her, Tony."

Laurel turned as if she had been stuck by a pin. Pamela—unforgettable, blond, ravishing Pamela—approached.

"I thought you were down on Geary Street." Tony looked surprised.

"I was, but we moved a month ago, and do you know that your nasty brother hasn't been here to see the gallery yet? It's always the winery this or the winery that, but he's coming this evening." Pamela tossed her head, her thick blond mane swinging seductively.

She seemed to be gloating over the fact that Vittorio was coming to see her, as if it were an achievement of sorts, and she had a unique way of making Laurel feel uncomfortable. This feeling was only intensified by Pamela's acknowledgement of her with, "Oh, hello there. Enjoying our city?"

"Yes, very much." Laurel resented the way Pamela seemed to take possession of things, even of San Francisco, and she moved toward the door.

"Oh, you bought one of those cute little posters." Pamela's tone reduced Laurel's poster to insignificance. Fortunately, Tony seemed just as inclined to leave.

"Perhaps you and"—Pamela hesitated—

"Laurie, would like to join us at Ernie's this evening?"

"Thanks, anyway," Tony replied, "but you can see we aren't dressed for Ernie's."

Laurel and Tony practically ran down the stairs, co-conspirators in their flight from Pamela's grasp. "Don't drop your cute little poster," Tony mimicked, and that sent both of them into peals of laughter.

"I have just the antidote for Pam and her gallery," Tony said. "There's an Impressionist exhibit on loan at the Palace of the Legion of Honor. We might catch it before closing."

At the museum, they ran from the parking lot, breezed by Rodin's larger-than-life sculpture in the courtyard, and hastily viewed the exhibit.

Coming out of the special exhibit, Laurel noticed an adjoining gallery filled with sculpture. She stared in disbelief at a study of Victor Hugo as he emerged from marble, only partially removed from the stone, and she turned and was captured instantly by a small work entitled, "The Kiss," two young figures in embrace.

The statue invited response, and she turned to Tony and said, "Oh, Vittorio—" She stopped, flustered, immediately correcting herself.

"Must have been a Freudian slip," Tony countered, pondering the statue, "but I have to admit that guy does look more like my muscleman brother than I."

They stood there a moment in silence, and images of Vittorio rotated in her mind. She turned away, once more reminded that Vittorio Bellini dominated her every perception.

CHAPTER FOUR

For the rest of the evening both Laurel and Tony were somewhat subdued. She suggested a quick hamburger on the way home because of the long working day tomorrow, and he seemed to understand. He deposited her at her door.

It had been a comfortable, friendly day. With Tony, she felt none of the sensations that his brother's presence always seemed to create. Thoughts of Vittorio, interwoven with the museum statue, played back in her mind, and she tried to erase them.

Surprised not to find Mooch in his usual waiting position on the porch, she went to the door and called. Why hadn't he come out to greet her in his overwhelming style? She called again, listened, and thought she heard a whimper—no, whine—coming from the back of the house. She called again and heard the same response and a soft bark.

The lights from the cottage spotlighted her way, and she found Mooch, straining to reach her, a rope tied to a tree impeding his progress. Thumbtacked to the trunk was an envelope. Trying to release Mooch from his captivity proved to be more difficult than she imagined. Whoever had tied the knot had done a more than thorough job. It would have held a Great Dane.

"It's all right, fellow. I'll have you loose in no time." She tried to hold the rope slack while attempting to work the knot. Finally Mooch was released, and he covered her with licks and climbed on her lap. He followed her to the house, where she let him come in. She settled in a chair to read the contents of the mysterious envelope, with Mooch contentedly sprawled at her feet.

The note was written with black felt pen that covered the page in a bold hand:

> *Maybe if you stay home, you could keep your dog under control. The new hybrid vines have been gnawed. Watch him or he'll have to go.*
>
> *V.*

The note was terse, rude, as if she had deliberately gone off and set Mooch on the vines. So far she had observed that Mooch's only interest in the vineyards was to chase a few rabbits away, a welcome function for a dog at a winery. Laurel could hardly believe that Mooch had gnawed the vines. And even if he was right, Vittorio could have informed her in another way, instead of this note scolding her as if she were a child.

To think that just a few minutes before she had been worried about her attraction to him! It seemed laughable. Vittorio had certainly provided the perfect coolant to her overwarm feelings. She would keep Mooch tied up tomorrow and ask Vittorio to explain further what had happened.

When Laurel approached the winery the next morning, the first gondola of Pinot Noir grapes was being poured into the crusher-stemmer, the wheels already set in motion for the crush. She entered the lab and could hear voices raised in anger, coming from Vittorio's office a few doors down.

"This hardly seems the appropriate moment to tell me this news." Vittorio's voice, hard and ironic, carried down the hallway.

"I didn't pick it. You did, with your little innuendoes about dating the help," Tony shouted. "I've been wanting to tell you for a long time, and your attitude has given me the courage. I'm not like you, Vittorio. I'm a different person—and as for dating, I'll date anyone I darn please!"

Laurel heard the slam of the outside office door and Tony depart. She stood there, not knowing what to do. Should she acknowledge that she had overheard? She could try to explain to Vittorio that she and Tony were just

friends, that she wouldn't see Tony again if
that would help. Or would it be best to ignore
the whole thing and attend to her job, which
was helping Emidio monitor all the activities
that were about to start at the winery? She
hesitated. Emidio emerged from the cellars,
calling her to come. She joined him, the decision postponed.

The routines that went with the harvest
were a continuing process, never a moment
to speak to Vittorio about anything. Days
and nights melted into weeks. The wine was
first in all thoughts—the grapes being
picked in succession, each grape in its own
setting maturing at a different time—and
everyone played a part. Laurel had never
been so tired, working almost around the
clock, visiting the cottage for a brief bite to
eat, a few hours of sleep, and then back on
the job.

Her encounters with Vittorio were brief
and businesslike. Whatever had transpired
between him and Tony was forgotten or at
least postponed until after the harvest, and
Mooch's indiscretion was forgotten.

The sound of the gondolas rolling out the
grapes and the beat of the crusher seemed a
part of her bones, echoing even in her rest-
less sleep. She sometimes felt she made her
rounds like a robot, wired to a task, checking
the temperature of the fermentations, super-
vising the racking as the wine moved from
one stage of development to another. To

Laurel, all life was on hold while the wine was in fermentation.

One morning Laurel climbed the ladder and walked the catwalk, checking the temperature of the reds, making certain it held to the temperature necessary for optimum fermentation. Too hot, and the mass would literally boil over. She could see Tony below, shouting directions, a load of pumice, dried grape skins, and pulp on its way to fertilize the fields. The last of the harvest was ended. Not that their work was finished, but finally there was at least a pause.

Laurel had an advantaged position from the catwalk. It was a view-from-an-attic sort of experience where she could peek out undetected and gain another perspective.

"Looks different up here, doesn't it?"

The voice was almost a whisper in her ear. She turned to acknowledge it and was a breath away from Vittorio, who made no effort to move back.

Laurel stood there stunned. Bending her head in an effort to avoid his eyes, she felt the touch of his fingertips under her chin. He gently raised her head until his gaze and hers were one. She saw the almond eyes in diffused focus now, and he kissed her. "My little tiger," he whispered.

His voice and the words brought Laurel to reality. She shoved him aside and fled to the ladder and to safety below. His voice behind her called, "Laurel," but she didn't hesitate, just continued her exodus from the cellars to the lab where Emidio, bent over his figures, hardly noticed her enter.

"Did you check the tanks?" Emidio asked her.

"I think the last of the reds is ready to draw off to the settling tanks."

"Good," he muttered. Then he looked up at Laurel. "Are you all right?"

"Yes," she lied. "Just a little faint."

"You've been working too hard. Go home now. You don't look well—get some sleep." Emidio looked at her with concern. "And I don't want to see you here tomorrow."

"Are you certain you can manage—"

"Go. Go." Emidio was up now and was almost sweeping her out the door. "Rest up," he called from the doorway.

Laurel released Mooch from his clothesline run and escorted him inside.

"What will I do, Mooch?" She sprawled across the bed. "What will I do?" she whispered to herself. Mooch seemed to sense her poignant mood and crawled up beside her. She pulled up the quilt at the end of the bed and curled up, hugging her pillow to her body, trying to wipe out the memory of the scene on the catwalk. A kiss? What did it mean? What should she do? Allowing the sedative of sleep to take over, she did nothing. *I'll decide tomorrow,* she thought. *Tomorrow.*

Laurel awakened to Mooch's soft bark, felt for the lamp beside her bed, fumbling around in the darkness that surrounded her, flipped it on, and checked the time—eight. She got up and brought Mooch a bowl of food, and for herself she took a salami from the refrigerator and whacked off a few hunks, which she placed on buttered French bread, and poured herself a glass of red wine.

Running through her mind were thoughts of the morning's encounter with Vittorio. She had wanted him to kiss her. In fact, just thinking about it made her realize that if it hadn't been for his teasing words, she would have forgotten who she was and that she was kissing her boss.

She was angry at herself and, yes, at Vittorio, too—after all his talk about not letting pleasure and business mingle. She had stayed away from Tony. They'd only shared some iced tea on her porch one afternoon. Vittorio had his nerve! Was this his way of testing her? Well, she had flunked. She knew that she must guard herself from getting into such a compromising position with him again.

Glancing in the corner, she spotted her flute case. She hadn't touched the instrument in months. She opened the case and pulled out the flute, assembled it, and began to play. Music always soothed her. It was comforting to have another sound in the cottage besides the murmuring of her own mind filled with problems she didn't know how to solve. The melancholy melody she played seemed to match her mood, and with concentration she did pretty well.

Mooch ran for the door and barked softly.

"You want out. That's not much of a compliment for my music. Well, okay, for a minute, but you'd better come right back when I call."

Laurel opened the door to let Mooch out and jumped back in alarm. She moved to slam the door, but an arm shot out and caught it.

"I didn't mean to frighten you," Vittorio explained.

"Well, you did," she replied. "Usually people knock when they come to call."

"I was mesmerized by the music. I didn't know you had so many other talents. May I come in?"

"Do I have a choice?"

"Well, if you're asking, no," he said as he pushed open the door and entered. "What you've done to the cottage is very nice."

"Thank you. But I'm sure that's not what you've come here to say."

"I've come to apologize." He grinned. "Well, not exactly to apologize, but to say that if this morning caused you any embarrassment, I want to explain that I'm not in the habit of—"

She interrupted him. "No need for explanations. We're adults. You needn't worry that I took it too seriously."

"Oh?" He looked puzzled, and then his eyes changed, as if a shutter had closed over them.

"Well, I meant that...that...it was just one of those things."

"Well, good." Vittorio's voice was icy. "I'm glad you consider it inconsequential. I wouldn't want there to be a misunderstanding between us."

Once again it was his eyes that flickered a warning, and Laurel felt any response superfluous.

"I guess then I'll apologize to Mooch. "I'm sorry," he said to the dog. "We caught another dog gnawing our vines. I accused you falsely." Mooch readily accepted Vittorio's offered handshake.

"Would you like some salami and a glass of wine?" Laurel moved to the table, out from under Vittorio's direct vision, and cut a hunk of salami.

"Salami isn't cut in hunks." Vittorio laughed and came up behind her. Taking the knife, he reached over her and sliced the salami paper thin. "This is the Italian way."

Laurel was wedged between Vittorio and the table, thankful that his hands, at least for now, were occupied with slicing the salami. "I think that's enough," she said in a voice grown faint.

"Quite right," he agreed, and let the knife

and salami drop on the table, putting his hands around her waist.

Laurel moved out of the position and poured him a glass of wine. Their fingers touched when she handed him the glass, and they remained motionless for a second. When Vittorio saw she was about to speak, he placed the fingers of one hand lightly on her mouth, as if to indicate silence. Her lips parted in what she thought was to be a protest, but her response was instead a gentle kiss to his fingertips, and he took her in his arms.

"No! No!" She hardly recognized her voice.

Vittorio stopped instantly. He looked at her, perplexed, and touched her hair, threading it through his fingers gently, as if it were a precious chain. "What's wrong, Laurel?"

"It's just not—" she started.

Mooch barked and then growled, going toward the door, and they heard a knock.

Laurel yelled at the door. "Who's there?"

"It's me—Tony. Are you okay? Emidio said—"

"Fine, but I'm too tired, and I just got out of the shower."

"Okay—I'll talk to you tomorrow and pick up my tie."

Laurel turned. Vittorio's eyes were riveted on Tony's red tie on the back of the chair. He had left it on the porch that hot day they'd shared iced tea.

"My little brother was never known for his perfect timing," he said sarcastically.

"Tony and I are just friends," she explained.

"Oh?" But Vittorio's voice implied more.

Laurel was furious at his implication. "What I do with my free time is my business, Mr. Bellini, and the first thing I'm doing is leaving this job."

"We have a contract, Laurel, but I won't hold you against your will. I have no quarrel with your job performance, and we do need you. I didn't mean to—"

"I'm tired of what you did or did not mean to." She moved to open the door. "Get out."

He stood, blocking her way. "If it's seeing me that's worrying you, don't concern yourself. I'll certainly keep my distance."

Laurel slammed the door after Vittorio and leaned against it, as if to prevent him from entering her life again. Angry, and frustrated by his insinuations, her first thought was to run away, but where? And running away was a childish impulse. Besides, she had made a commitment until January, and Emidio needed her.

She felt trapped here now, trapped by her need for the job, by her commitment, and— she had to admit—by a need to prove herself to Vittorio. Contact with him had left her rife with confusion. He was a hotheaded Italian who jumped to conclusions, who obviously showed no understanding of her. She had her

pride, too, and it didn't include being
stomped on. Before this was over, she vowed
to have the last word. She wouldn't run
away—that would be too easy for him.

By now the tears were running down her
face, and Mooch was looking very mournful.
She went to the sink and washed her swollen
eyes with a cold compress. She held up her
glass of wine in a mock toast.

"I won't be defeated by this!"

Now that she was in control, she was
grateful for Tony's interruption. She thought
of her college boyfriend, Rick, and their easy
friendship, of Tony, and of how different and
complicated it all seemed with Vittorio. What
was it he called her—"tiger"? Then why did
she feel like a vulnerable kitten?

She latched the door, turned off the lights
in the front room, and went into the bedroom.
The red tie, a painful reminder, was still on
the chair. She folded it and placed it in a
drawer, out of sight.

Late the next day Tony dropped by. "Emidio said you were exhausted."

"I was pretty tired."

"How are you feeling now?"

"Much better, thanks." She hoped she
looked better than she felt.

"You're doing a good job, Laurel."

"Thanks."

"Even Vittorio is pleased. I can tell."

"I'm not so sure."

"I know, he can be difficult, but he doesn't

mean to be. It's just this place means so much to him. I told him I wanted to live in San Francisco. At first he had a fit. I think he's beginning to understand, but I haven't hit him with the real problem."

Laurel looked up, surprised. "The real problem?"

"Yep—I'm in love." Tony looked at her intently.

Laurel had a momentary concern. Was Tony thinking he was in love with her? She liked Tony, but love? She tried to interrupt him. "Sometimes people think they're in love and—"

"Oh, I know it." Tony was emphatic. "I've always known it, and Julie feels the same way about me—at least I think so."

"What do you mean, you think so? Haven't you told her?"

"Well, not in so many words."

Laurel was relieved. Of course, it all added up—Tony was in love with someone named Julie. "Well, what's the problem?"

"It's Julie Calomeni. It's always been understood that Julie would marry Vittorio. That's the way it is with families. The Calomenis own the property next to ours, a smaller operation but a respected winery too."

"This is the twentieth century, Tony. Families don't arrange marriages anymore."

"You don't understand, Laurel. It's just one of those silent assumptions. Julie's away at college, but she graduates in June, and she'll be home for Thanksgiving vacation. There's more at stake here—it's the blending of two wine-making families, and you know how Vittorio feels about the wine."

"But you're his brother, so what difference does that make?"

"I know, but Julie and Vittorio did date once in a while, and what if he's seriously interested in her?"

Laurel could see something of the problem, but Vittorio was obviously attracted to Pamela and had some interest in Laurel herself, hardly the behavior of a man promised to someone else. Was she just an interlude in his affections?

"I'm sure you'll find a way to tell Vittorio, but first you have to settle this with Julie." She took Tony's hands in hers to reassure him.

"I know. Maybe I'm making problems where there aren't any."

The Ferrari came down the drive and screeched to a stop in front of the cottage. Laurel dropped Tony's hands, shocked to see Pamela behind the wheel.

"How are you two?" Pam said it in a tone that implied they were twin cocker spaniels. "I begged Vitto to let me drive it around the loop. Isn't it divine?"

Laurel and Tony watched her turn at the bottom of the drive and circle toward the house.

"Where did she come from?" Laurel asked.

"Out of the woodwork, I guess." Tony laughed. "I've never known Vittorio to let anyone drive his car before, even for a few minutes."

Pamela was very persuasive, Laurel thought. Persuasive enough to win Vittorio's permanent affection?

They looked at the top of the drive to see Pamela get in the passenger side and Vittorio climb behind the wheel. The figures were barely distinguishable when the car passed. Pamela's wave was fleeting, and Laurel was left with the feeling she'd been dismissed.

CHAPTER FIVE

Laurel made certain that Tony took his tie before he left that afternoon. She promised him to meet Julie when she came home, then wondered if it was wise. *Surely,* she thought, *just meeting the girl doesn't make me an accessory to the marriage. Why do things have a way of getting so complicated?*

Sunday she got up early, reveling in a whole day to herself. She put on her jogging shorts and shoes and set out. After a short jog to the top of the vineyards, she was winded and could feel the pull in her legs.

She sat looking down on the vineyards, the twisted limbs now free of grapes. The pruners would attack those limbs in a few weeks, cutting away the dormant wood and extra shoots to ensure optimum performance for the next growing season. If only she could shed the extraneous in her life so easily! At least, for the present, Vittorio had been pruned out.

She tried to assess what she knew so far about Vittorio. She knew him to be a man of decision, strength, integrity, and responsibility in the community. She knew he would stand by his beliefs even if they were not profitable or popular, and she had seen him nurture the vines with care and tenderness. He exuded masculinity, but on occasion seemed almost vulnerable in his needs. Unpredictable? Unreasonable?

And she could not forget Pamela. And what about Julie? Would Tony be a match for Vittorio? Laurel couldn't imagine anyone resisting Vittorio, and this realization suddenly caused her to consider—could she be in love with this man? She pushed the thought aside. Impossible. She didn't need or want any part of that.

She must remember that he was her boss, and so far their encounters had ended in pain. She had worked hard for her independence and professionalism; she wasn't about to give them up. Attraction wasn't necessarily love.

Laurel made her decision—to stay only until the end of her contract. Staying beyond that would be tempting fate. It would be awkward enough as it was.

Vittorio was not at the winery the next day, and Laurel was relieved to discover he would not be back until Tuesday. She went about her duties and was grateful that she didn't have to worry about avoiding him.

On Vittorio's return, he called Emidio, Tony, and her into his office. Laurel noted that he looked tanned and rested from wherever he had been. He gave her a quick, steely glance that seemed to say, *Well, I see you're still here.* She met the challenge of his eyes without flinching.

"I'm breaking a precedent this year," Vittorio began. "Tony and Pamela have convinced me that I must be more modern in my marketing techniques, so I've gone along with the idea of a festival, or rather a reception, here at the winery, the first Sunday in December. We'll introduce our new, popularly priced white wine, which will be ready in the marketplace for the holidays. We'll preview it for buyers, critics, and our faithful customers and neighbors, numbering some one hundred people or so. We'll have an art exhibit for the public to view for a month—California artists featured, both old and new. What do you think?"

And, without waiting for an answer, he continued, "Tony, you'll take care of the invitations and releases.

"Laurel, you'll work with Pamela and be in charge of the catering. I feel you women have more of a feel for that—and perhaps you could play your flute," he said pointedly to Laurel.

"Have you picked a name for the wine?" Emidio asked.

"Not yet, but I'm open to suggestions."

Tony was enthusiastic about the plan and

immediately started to discuss his ideas, while Laurel sat in her chair, speechless, irritation combined with dismay at having to handle the added responsibilities, which might place her in further contact with Vittorio.

Reason told her it was a good idea, a great one for the winery, and it was evident Vittorio needed all their help to make it a success. Laurel brooded over this while she checked the alcohol, acids, and sulphur contents in the wines and monitored the secondary fermentations. This was her job. She was a winemaker, not a public relations director, but she had to admit that in an operation like this, sometimes jobs did overlap.

Playing the flute? She wasn't obligated to do that, nor would she. But music and wine were like cheese and wine. Yes, she would find others to play—wandering minstrel types, two flutists in peasant dress. Yes, it was a perfect idea, and she got caught up in the festival plans in spite of herself.

Pamela appeared several days later to consult with Laurel. She had her instructions from Vittorio, too, and was her usual overbearing self.

"We'll hang the contemporaries over here" —she pointed to the rock-wall columns between the window—"and the older paintings here,"—indicating a painted wall to the left of the entrance.

Laurel concentrated on her surroundings.

The bar was a complete circle in the center of the almost circular room. The windows, each pictures complete in themselves, were divided by the rock. It seemed a shame to detract from them.

Laurel made an effort to be tactful. "The wall is a good idea, Pamela, but can't we come up with something besides the rock? Don't you think that—"

"I think I know more about hanging paintings than you do," Pam interrupted defensively.

"Well, I was thinking that the long hallway that leads into this room would be a more—"

"Yes." It was Vittorio, standing in the doorway.

Pam looked up, startled, momentarily frowned, and quickly recovered. "I was just about to suggest that as an alternative—a brilliant idea, Vitto." She went to him and took his arm. "Yes, the contemporaries would be better against this more neutral background."

For a moment Laurel almost felt sorry for Pamela, who was being forced to agree with her. Laurel felt a surge of pity toward her. "It's Pam's idea to use this wall for the older paintings," Laurel conceded.

"Good," was Vittorio's only comment, which sent Pamela into a radiant smile. "Well, I'll leave you women to your work."

Why did he say things like that? It was

like waving a red flag in Laurel's face. Didn't he know he was baiting her?

Pamela didn't appear the least bit fazed by his remark. Laurel wondered if she was plastic.

"I had a devil of a time getting Vittorio to agree to use these paintings." Pamela took a tape and started to measure the wall areas. "Vitto tells me you'll be leaving in January." The remark was meant as a barb.

Laurel wondered what else "Vitto" had discussed with Pamela, and it was difficult to cover her dismay. Well, he was right; she did intend to leave. Laurel pretended she hadn't heard her.

"Can you take care of the food arrangements, Laurel? It's just that I'll be so busy with the pictures, and you'll be here on the scene, so to speak."

"Fine with me." Laurel had already given the menu some thought. She preferred to manage it alone.

Pamela rattled on, "An orchestra would be nice, black tie, and shrimp, lots of shrimp. I wonder what I should wear."

Laurel's mind was elsewhere. She could already see the round tables along one side of the room, with baskets of rust and yellow mums and ivory tapers flickering and reflecting in the windows. On the tables would be baskets of French bread and cheeses in rounds partially sliced, their mellow colors on wooded boards adding texture to the design decor. Circulating the crowd would be waitresses in simple fall print skirts and peasant blouses, passing hot hors d'oeuvres, and behind the bar the wine would be served to be sampled by Vittorio's guests. It was a friendly, warm picture, and she was caught up short when she heard Pamela ask, "Are you sure you'll be able to manage?"

Laurel looked up. "No problem." She smiled.

"Don't hesitate to call," was Pamela's off-handed remark as she breezed out the door.

Vittorio said that Laurel was in charge, so in charge she would be. She hoped that her vision of the evening was what he had in mind. Well, he had left this "women's work" to her, and she would make the decisions. He had indicated she had free rein, and she intended to take it.

She was an organizer, and although the festival responsibilities were considerable, she listed all she must arrange for and found time in the space of her days or evenings to make contacts, interview caterers, and line up things.

Summoning up the courage to speak to Vittorio, she went to him one afternoon. She stood before his door a few moments before knocking.

"Yes." His voice was coming not from inside but from behind her. His unexpected position caught her off guard, and she whirled around.

"Can I help you with something?" Vittorio asked.

"I thought you should know what I've been doing."

"And just what have you been up to?"

"About the festival," she made it clear.

"Do you have something to show me?"

Everything Vittorio said seemed to imply more than one meaning to Laurel. She hadn't been this close to him since that night, and she backed away.

"Here." She thrust the papers at him.

He checked the orders and nodded. "Fine."

"Don't you want to know the details?"

"It looks as if you know what you're doing," he said calmly.

"But—"

"I'm grateful that you decided to stay."

"I felt I didn't have much choice," she quipped back and then regretted her biting words. Why did she always end up sparring with him even when he seemed to be paying her a compliment?

"Everyone always has the freedom to choose, Laurel."

"I'm not a quitter."

"Nor am I," he said and quietly brushed past her into his office and closed the door.

Laurel stared at the closed door. She'd been dismissed. He always had the last word.

She returned to the security of the lab to find Emidio at his desk, his body hunched over some paperwork.

"This time, it's my turn," Laurel insisted. "Emidio, go home and rest, please."

"I am unusually tired, but do you think you can manage?"

"I know where I can find you, and I promise to call if I need you."

Emidio rose from his chair with great effort, and Laurel helped him on with his sweater. "Maybe you should see a doctor, Emidio, just to be sure."

"No, no. It's nothing. I'm just tired. With a little rest I'll be good as new," he reassured her.

Laurel watched him go to his car, concerned at the absence of the usual spring in his step. He backed out and headed for his home, which was on the other side of the property.

She had grown very fond of that gentle soul. He lived alone now since his wife's death a few years ago. She'd check on him later, after she put the winery to bed for the night.

The papers on Emidio's desk lay in disarray, as if they had been shuffled aimlessly, not his usual style. Sorting through the forms, she stacked what appeared to be related together and gave the desk a semblance of its accustomed order. *He's even left behind his beloved pipe,* Laurel thought. Maybe she was overreacting, but that was really out of character for Emidio. Hesitating for only a moment, she headed for Vittorio's office.

In her anxiety Laurel forgot about knocking. Vittorio looked up, startled. "People usually knock when they come to call," he said in a mocking voice and quickly changed his tone. "What's wrong?"

"It's Emidio."

Vittorio leaped from his chair and moved toward the door.

"It's not an emergency," she explained, "but he didn't look well, and I sent him home. Maybe I shouldn't have let him go alone. It's just a feeling I have—his desk's a mess, and he even left this." She showed him the pipe.

Grabbing the pipe, Vittorio went out the door, calling, "I'll let you know after I check on him."

Fortunately she and Emidio had discussed what needed to be done that afternoon. Although Laurel was learning fast, she relied on Emidio's expertise for direction. When she walked through the cellars, she felt diminished by them. When Emidio was with her, she felt in charge.

Now, without the security of his presence, the giant tanks and barrels in the dimmed light seemed menacing. The stainless-steel holding tanks were particularly less friendly, she thought. She felt more at home with the stacks of smaller wooden cooperage that emitted the faint odor of wine and oak.

Completing her tasks, she went back to the lab, anxious for Vittorio's call. She washed all the glassware until it shone and jumped when the phone finally did ring.

"He seems okay, but I've run him over to Dr. Luke's just to be sure. Under full protest, but we're here. I'm with you—he certainly doesn't look his usual self. How are things going there?"

"No problem."

"Fine." And he hung up.

Later, at the cottage, Laurel prepared a small casserole to take over to Emidio's. Even if he didn't want to eat it tonight, he could put it in the freezer for another time. Besides, it made her feel as if she were doing something. The leftover chicken in a cream sauce with artichoke hearts was one of her favorites.

The phone rang, and she picked up the receiver almost instantly.

"You must have been sitting on the phone." At the sound of Vittorio's relaxed voice, Laurel knew that things with Emidio must be all right. "The doctor says it's just fatigue. Emidio says it's indigestion. The prescription is complete rest for several days and then a more relaxed schedule for a while."

Laurel could hear Emidio in the background saying, "Tell her I'll be back tomorrow."

"Ignore him," Vittorio said, laughing.

"I've made a casserole. Do you think—"

"Good, we're starving."

On the drive over to Emidio's, Laurel

couldn't help thinking that Vittorio and she had actually had what one would call a normal conversation without innuendoes, without sarcasm. True, it had been only a few sentences, but that was progress.

Laurel carefully picked up the casserole and admired the wide, covered front porch, complete with old-fashioned porch swing. An apron-clad Vittorio opened the door before she reached it and held the screen door aside for her to enter. Emidio was sitting on the sofa, pillows at his back, feet up, covered with an afghan, and Vittorio was bustling about him protectively.

"Will you call him off?" Emidio pleaded. "I think he's missed his calling. He should have been a nurse."

"You know, you did give us a bit of a scare," Laurel said.

"Can't a man get tired?"

"Tired, but not tired out. I mean to see you follow the doctor's orders." Vittorio was emphatic.

Emidio held up his hands in surrender and smiled.

Laurel noticed that Vittorio had thrown a checkered tablecloth over the cocktail table in front of the sofa. On it were set three places and in the middle a single candle in a brass holder.

"I made the salad." He looked pleased with himself.

"Great," she said. "Just a few minutes in the oven, and this will be warm again."

Vittorio headed for the kitchen with her casserole in hand, and she was alone with Emidio.

"You will follow the doctor's instructions," she told him.

"Of course. I'm no fool, but he said that in a few days I can go back. I have full confidence in your abilities to manage things while I'm gone."

"As do I," Vittorio said, entering the room. "It won't be easy to get along without you, Emidio, but we'll manage. The main thing is for you to get completely rested."

"I'll drink to that." Emidio lifted his glass, and Vittorio filled each of their glasses with a clear white wine, almost crystal clear. Laurel tasted the delicate wine. It was unfamiliar to her—dry, with just a hint of sweet, so light and with a touch of effervescence.

Emidio looked at Vittorio. "It's the new wine."

"Yes, I thought this a fitting occasion. I had one of the men bring it over."

"It's all I thought it would be."

"To Emidio, to the birth of a new wine." Vittorio lifted his glass.

"It's so clear, really a lovely wine," Laurel remarked.

"Clear enough to see the color of your eyes reflected in it," Vittorio said.

Emidio added, "Yes, and yours too, Vittorio."

Laurel looked at Vittorio, who held his glass at eye level. The dark almond eye seemed to be memorizing her, and she lowered her glass so that she was longer looking through the glass but down at it.

"I smell the casserole," she said.

Vittorio dashed off to the kitchen once again.

"He's quite domestic," Laurel said, laughing.

Emidio laughed with her, and she didn't know why it struck them both so funny, but they were still laughing when Vittorio appeared again.

"What's the joke?"

"Well, it's just that we never thought of you as being such a fine domestic," Emidio replied.

Vittorio made a mock bow from the waist. "Just trying to be at your service. And now, are you ready for dinner to be served?" He made a sweeping gesture with his hand, flicking his apron to one side. Emidio and Laurel both nodded their heads and continued to laugh.

"This is no laughing matter, I assure you." Vittorio went over and turned out the lights. He groped his way to the cocktail table and lit the candle. "Voilà—light."

"This is almost too much for a sick man," Emidio exclaimed.

The whole room took on another dimension by candlelight. Vittorio had created a festive occasion out of what could have been just a depressing day. Indicating where Laurel was to sit, he refilled the glasses with wine, returned with the tossed salad, the casserole, and a few slices of French bread.

"I think I should have a collapse more often," Emidio remarked. "I can't remember when I last had such a good time."

"Nor better food," Vittorio said.

After dinner Laurel and Vittorio worked side by side in the kitchen while Emidio got into bed.

"I thought I'd stay the night," Vittorio whispered.

"That's a good idea,"

"He doesn't think it's necessary, but I think he protests too much."

"I can hear you two out there talking about me," Emidio called out.

"We're only saying things we wouldn't dare say in front of you. I'm going to see Laurel to her car."

"That's all right—I can manage." Laurel picked up her empty dish.

"I know you can manage," Vittorio countered. "I want to."

On the porch, out of earshot of Emidio, he indicated the swing. He sat down beside her, gently putting the swing in motion.

"You don't see these often."

"Only in movies," she said.

"Laurel, I hate to bring this up now, but I must talk a little business. I'm asking you to stay a little longer than your contract."

"I don't know. I'd like to, but—"

"Before you answer, hear me out. I know now that I haven't always been fair to you. I've been wrong about...." He paused. "I'm not known for my even temper and...." He paused again. "I want to clear—"

Laurel interrupted, accepting his attempt at an apology. "Perhaps we could forget some of what's happened."

"We need you, Laurel."

"I'll stay for a while."

"Thank you."

"There's no need to thank me, Vittorio. I love my work here."

He placed his arm tentatively around her shoulders. Laurel tensed a little, but she didn't draw away, and he didn't seem to press his attentions on her, so she relaxed against the back of the swing.

"Will you join us for Thanksgiving dinner? Angie would be so pleased if you would."

The motion of the swing combined with the wine put Laurel in a relaxed frame of mind. "Yes, Vittorio."

All she could hear was the creak of the swing and the silence of the darkness that surrounded them. The rhythm of the swing seemed to repeat the phrase in her head, *Yes, Vittorio ... yes, Vittorio ... yes, Vittorio.*

Completely relaxed now, her head rested lightly on Vittorio's shoulder. His voice called her name and seemed to cover her in soft folds. "Laurel, Laurel."

He kissed her, and she opened her eyes. She couldn't perceive his face, so close to hers now. She placed her hands between them, gently pushing him away. "Vittorio, please." Her voice was faint.

"Laurel, don't deny what you're feeling."

"You don't understand."

"I know how I feel about you."

"That's not enough, Vittorio."

"And just what are your requirements?"

"You're being unfair."

"I already admitted to that."

"I don't think this conversation is getting us anywhere. Haven't I agreed to stay to help at the winery?"

"This has nothing to do with the winery," he emphasized.

"What I mean is—" She hesitated. "We hardly know each other."

"I know all I need to know, Laurel, and I've never felt quite like this before. You needn't be afraid—"

Laurel didn't let him finish the sentence. "Afraid?" She stood up and moved toward the stairs. "Not afraid, Vittorio—undecided."

"I can wait." He stated it as a simple fact, like the conclusion was already drawn, and then, as an afterthought, he added, "Is there anyone else?"

"No."

"It wouldn't really matter much if there were, my little tiger." This time he said it without rancor, just complete confidence, escorting her to the car in silence.

CHAPTER SIX

The implications of the conversation were enough to keep Laurel awake the entire night, tossing and turning, going over and over what was said and what was left unsaid. Vittorio had made it plain that he was serious about his interest in her and that it would be only a matter of time before she would return his affection. If he only knew how thin that edge was!

He was right when he said she couldn't deny her feelings. Then why was she sitting on her bed, clutching her pillow in desperation, unsuccessful in her attempt to push away the memory of his touch? She could hear his voice murmuring, "Laurel, Laurel."

She tossed aside the pillow and got up and heated some warm milk. She changed into a warmer flannel gown with a high neck and long sleeves and wrapped her robe around her, letting the warm milk soothe her inner panic.

Was she afraid? Rick had said it, too—"What are you afraid of, Laurel?" But with Rick it hadn't been fear. She knew that now—it had been disinterest. Was that why she had allowed the relationship to continue so long? Its safety? Yet, when Rick had walked out of her life, she had been lonely, so lonely that she had vowed never to be dependent on anyone again.

She remembered the fear that followed her father's death. She had felt herself floundering, as if she would be unable to function without his support and counsel, which had always been a steady current in her life, but she had.

Sprawled on her bed, in the twilight zone between sleep and consciousness, Laurel saw herself reaching for Vittorio, reaching for her father, and finding no one there. She heard herself scream, and she awakened.

Mooch growled and barked, jumped onto the bed and lapped her face as if to reassure her that she was still all there. And Laurel, wide-eyed now, knew that she was afraid of all that loving Vittorio would ask of her, of loving too much and not being loved in return, of disappearing in that love and being left with nothing.

Vittorio hadn't mentioned love or commitment. And there was still the question of Pamela and Julie. Surely he couldn't be....

Something had resolved his doubt of her involvement with Tony, but they hadn't discussed it. *We need to talk some of this out.* Well, he said he could wait, and so could she.

Handling Emidio's duties at the winery in addition to her own kept Laurel unbelievably busy. Tony helped, and Vittorio came to the lab each morning, perching his dominating form on one of the high stools, lingering over his mug of coffee. In this setting she felt warmed and comforted by his appearances and easily able to communicate with him about what was going on.

"I need Emidio for the blending," she told him.

"He can come back tomorrow for a couple of hours, and we'll share in the input. Of course, he has the final say. Why don't you run some samplings, talk to him on the phone? I'm sure he can guide you. You're managing things very well."

"Thank heaven Emidio is as close as the telephone."

No mention was made of their conversation on the porch swing. Vittorio's actions were somewhat proprietary, but Laurel understood this. The winery was his dominion, and she was part of the operation.

When the Ferrari came up the drive the next day at an unnaturally slow speed, Laurel smiled because she realized that Vittorio was holding back because of his special cargo. He rushed to help Emidio out, and Emidio waved him off with an irritated gesture.

"Really, I'm not about to break."

Laurel had hastily scratched out a *Welcome Home* sign on the back of some paper towels. Emidio acknowledged the sign with a what-am-I-to-do gesture that brought laughter to them all. She gave him a report on her activities, and he was especially gratified that she had done some of the statistic gathering required by the government.

The wine samples were lined up, each in its own breaker, formulas noted. Laurel, Vittorio, and Emidio tasted each sampling, comparing appearances, aroma, bouquet, body, and flavor, and other qualities. It was for the fitness of their judgment that men like Emidio were known throughout the industry. It took several hours of back-and-forth tasting and notations, and Emidio was still not satisfied. He went over to one blend and added what looked to Laurel as an infinitesimal more Petite Sirah. They tasted, and Laurel clapped. This was it.

"A blend is like a good marriage, bringing the best qualities of each to create something new." Emidio looked thoughtful. "It was like that for Margaret and me."

"That's enough for your first day back," Vittorio admonished.

"Go away and leave me to Laurel," Emidio retorted. "Go back to your office. Anyone would think you were afraid to leave me alone with her. We have things to talk about."

Laurel noted that Emidio was the only one who could talk to Vittorio like that and produce a smile.

"I can see that rest has done nothing for your disposition. Call me when you're ready to return, and don't be too long." Vittorio headed down the hall.

Emidio gave Laurel detailed instructions on what to do, how to handle the blending of the large lots. Glancing at his watch, he said, "I guess I'd better call the young lion, or he'll drag me out of here bodily. There's only so far that you can push Vittorio before it becomes dangerous."

Left to her work, Laurel put on her jacket and went into the cellars. Tomorrow was Thanksgiving, and she had offered to make pumpkin pies for Angie, so that was to be a long day.

She directed the transfer of the first of the four reds that would make up the new wine to be racked out of their oak homes of a year. The large, empty redwood tank was waiting for its new inhabitant, cleaned and sterilized. Concentrating on the formula and standing beside the large tank, she felt a cool wetness, and before she could realize what was happening, she was being rained on in red. She screamed, and the rained-on effect ceased, but her feet were being rapidly covered in the same color, the racking hose completely broken now.

Laurel shouted for someone to turn off the pump and valve, but in just a few moments a substantial amount of the beautiful red liquid ran down the drain in the floor. Even in her sodden state, her concern was for the wine. She inspected the hose, directed its replacement, and started to help with washing down the area.

"Parfum de Burgundy." Vittorio was standing beside her. "My favorite scent."

"Laugh, and you may join me," she threatened, pointing the water dangerously in his direction.

"A little water never hurt anyone." In one quick movement he had grabbed the water hose and directed it on her. "You need a little washing down," he said, laughing.

Laurel sputtered and lunged forward and tried to take possession of the hose again. In the struggle Vittorio, too, was getting his share of dunking. She slipped, and in an effort to catch her, he broke her fall and slithered to the floor beside her—wine and water. Vittorio and Laurel.

He helped her to her feet. "You're shivering," he noted.

"That's what people usually do when they're covered with cold water in a cold place," Laurel remarked, and she felt herself being scooped up into his arms.

"I've got a shower in the office."

"I'd prefer to go to the cottage."

"Nonsense. You must get warmed right away."

In the office, still holding her, he pretended to lick the wine on her cheek.

"My, what a tasty blend!" he teased.

"Vittorio, you're enjoying my discomfort."

"Now, Laurel, that's too harsh."

"I've got nothing to put on."

"Good!" And then he added quickly, "I'll find something suitable." He set her down and pushed her toward the shower door.

"And what about you?"

"Would you like me to join you?" He stepped toward the door, and she slammed it in his face and bolted it.

"I'll be back in a few minutes," Vittorio yelled, and Laurel was comforted when she heard the door of the office close.

Laurel stripped herself of her clothes and got under the shower. The hot water did feel good and she shivered again—not from the cold, but from remembering Vittorio's warmth as he carried her—remembering, too, that she hadn't been in a hurry to have him put her down.

She rubbed her hair almost dry and wrapped a small towel in a turban around it. A larger towel formed a sarong, and she sat, as dignified as she could, on top of the "john," waiting for Vittorio to return with, she hoped, something dry and concealing. A few minutes later she heard the latch click.

"Is that you?"

"None other."

She opened the bathroom door a small crack, and Vittorio tossed something into her hands. She closed the door, only to notice a bikini about the size of a postage stamp.

"Is this your idea of funny?" she yelled.

"I thought that since you had just gone swimming—" He was roaring with laughter now. "It was something that was left at the pool."

"Vittorio, if you don't get me something else and quick, I will put on this thing and march right out of here into the cellar and put on a show for the crew. And just how would that look?"

"A benefit not in their contracts," he answered. "We can't have that." He knocked. "Here."

This time she was given a warm terry robe that truly concealed her. *It must be his,* she thought, and she wondered how she must appear with the sleeves rolled, extending beyond her hands, and the length dragging, difficult to manage without tripping. She could smell the scent of him in the fabric, and she wrapped it around her as tightly as she could. Stepping out of the bathroom, she saw warmth and caring reflected in his eyes— and what appeared to be admiration in spite of her bedraggled appearance.

"Stop looking at me like that and take me home."

"And how am I looking at you?"

"Well, not as if you were admiring my brain."

"I do." He laughed. "That, too."

She clutched her wet clothes to her as a buffer between them.

"For Pete's sake, you'll get all wet again," he warned.

"Then for Pete's sake, take me home!" Barefooted, she marched toward the Ferrari, robe dragging behind her.

"You're not getting in there all wet. Is nothing sacred?"

Once again she found herself in his arms. Once again she had to acknowledge that she liked it there. He carried her down the drive and deposited her on the porch.

"Aren't you worried about appearances?" she asked. "I must look pretty ridiculous, wrapped up in your robe and being carried down a hill in broad daylight."

"Not ridiculous, Laurel—enchanting." He wrapped his arms around her, and even through the thick robe she could feel his heart beat. Her head gently pressed against his chest, and his voice soothed, "Oh, little tiger." It was a comforting tone. "I never meant to embarrass you." He released her quickly, and Laurel felt chilled without his touch. "As you like," he said, and turned his back and strode away.

She picked up her wet clothes heaped on the porch. Once inside, she dressed and put her clothes to soak in the kitchen sink. She hung his robe on a hanger to dry.

A letter in her mailbox brought unwanted news. It was from Rick, asking if he could see her. All she needed right now was to resurrect an old romance! She put his letter on her pile of unanswered correspondence.

She forced herself to have a cup of soup and a piece of toast. She rolled out the pie dough, the sound of the rolling pin moving on the board. She did everything to make the pies automatically, fretfully. It wasn't until they were cooling on a rack that she began to relax.

Thanksgiving Day was one of those perfect fall days—cool, crisp, yet the sun was shining. She placed the pies in a carton and balanced them carefully on her trip to the chateau. Visions of pumpkin smeared all over the pavement cautioned her to make two trips.

"Thank you, Laurel." Angie's appreciation was evident. "They're beautiful and a big help. I wonder every Thanksgiving how I'm going to get all this food prepared and then if there's enough—and there's always too much. I don't know why I fret about it. You wouldn't think I'd ever cooked a Thanksgiving meal before." And then to Laurel's amazement Angie broke down in tears.

"Forgive me," Angie said, wiping her eyes. "It's nothing."

Laurel put her arms around her.

"It's just that this is the first Thanksgiving here since the accident, and Elise Calomeni is gone, too—so many absent." Angie dabbed her eyes, gaining control of herself. "And I want things to go well. It will be difficult for the boys."

"I'll be up to help you in a few minutes." Laurel gave her a quick hug. Of course, she thought, why hadn't she been sensitive to that? It was particularly difficult to handle the holidays after the death of someone you loved. Laurel remembered the pain of that first Christmas without her father, that hollow feeling that no amount of festivity managed to fill.

"Difficult for the boys." Laurel smiled at the phrase. Vittorio and Tony were hardly what one could call "boys," but to Angie, yes—"boys." She neatened the cottage and debated whether to dress for dinner now or later, deciding that after a day in the kitchen, later would make more sense. She fed Mooch and grabbed an apron.

Even before she reached the kitchen door, the smells announced that the turkey was already cooking. She peered into the oven.

"It looks gorgeous," Laurel enthused. "Now what would you like me to do?"

"If you could set the table," Angie replied.

"How many?" Laurel asked.

"Let's see...the Calomenis, Emidio..."

Angie counted to herself. "Eight." She showed Laurel where the china, glasses, and linens were kept.

"Do you have any preference?" Laurel was impressed with what she had to work with. Maria Bellini must have given her tables a great deal of thought.

"No, you decide," Angie directed on her way back to the kitchen.

Table coverings of damask, lace, and linen, three sets of china, and cranberry glasses and Waterford crystal, made Laurel's decision difficult. With two leaves in the table, there would be plenty of room for eight. She selected the Waterford and a white damask cloth.

The china seemed to depict the harvest, with the shades of greens, browns, reds, and rusts fused delicately in a floral pattern about the edges. She selected napkins to complement these colors and found some dried wheat stalks and Indian corn, arranging these in an informal bouquet amid mums and berries picked from the garden. Silver candelabra added to the elegant picture, but not so elegant, Laurel thought, as to be intimidating. She stood back and admired her work, bending to add a few more greens to the bottom of the centerpiece.

"Once again I must thank you." Vittorio stood in the doorway. "Is this your work?" he asked.

Laurel nodded, hoping he would like it.

She looked up and noticed that his eyes were filled with tears.

Vittorio cleared his throat. "Quite lovely." He hurried into the kitchen.

"Umm." It was Vittorio's voice, presumably admiring something in preparation.

She could hear Angie's immediate protest. "Get your hands out of there. There won't be anything left for the guests. Out, out of my kitchen!" And the tiny Angie shoved him out the kitchen door.

"It seems I'm not welcome in there." Vittorio was smiling now.

"Not unless you want to work," Laurel invited.

"I know when I'm outnumbered." He laughed and departed down the hallway.

"The table is beautiful," Angie remarked. "Maria took great pride in her tables. Thank you, Laurel. She would be pleased with this one."

"She would be pleased," was a phrase that Laurel had heard before. Without ever having known Maria Bellini, Laurel knew she would have liked her. Her physical presence was absent, but her memory was very much alive in the hearts of those who knew and loved her, still a part of every life she had touched.

"I've got it all pretty well under control." Angie stirred something simmering on the stove. "For the pasta," she explained. "This Thanksgiving will have an Italian touch. I guess it will be different from what you're used to."

"A little," Laurel agreed, "but it doesn't look as if I'll be suffering from any lack of good food." They sat across the small kitchen table, drinking coffee, while Laurel shared her childhood memories of past Thanksgivings with her family.

From the cottage she put in a call to her mother and then her brother. After hanging up, she thought of all the things she should have told them. That always seemed to be the way. When she was on the phone, all she could manage to say was, "Is everything all right? I love you," and that was about it. But they did discuss plans for a family reunion during the Christmas holidays. Just hearing their voices had made her feel better, but had also kindled a desire to see them.

Laurel dressed in a jade-green silk, with a single strand of pearls around her neck. She put on her highest heels, noticing they were made in Italy. *Well, at least my shoes are insiders,* she thought.

CHAPTER SEVEN

Vittorio's obviously approving glance on her entrance made Laurel glad of the extra attention she had given her appearance. Pam was dressed in a soft blue creation that shouted out its designer label, hugging every curve tastefully. Laurel had to confess that Pam enhanced the dress, her golden hair gleaming in the sun's soft reflections in the window.

Sherry was being poured from the decanter on the small marble table, the same decanter that Laurel shared that first night at the Bellinis', a night, when measured in happenings, that seemed years ago.

Emidio came forward with a glass for Laurel. "Quite a change from your usual working clothes, but I would have recognized you." His eyes twinkled.

At the sound of the bell, Tony went quickly to the door, and in the rush of greetings

Laurel gathered that the Calomenis had arrived. The older man, Sam Calomeni, was of medium height, gray haired, with a round, affable countenance. When he shook her hand, she noticed he had the hands of a workingman, creased, stubby fingers that felt strong and powerful. He was followed by his son, John, handsome, lean, tall, with quite a studious expression, and his daughter, Julie.

Julie was exquisite, an Italian Madonna, olive skinned, with dark, curly hair, and large, dark eyes and lashes that dominated her face, giving her a look of innocence and vulnerability.

She greeted Laurel with open friendliness. "I've heard a lot of nice things about you."

Laurel thought that Julie and John must have looked like their late mother, Elise, since they had little resemblance to their more rugged-featured father.

Laurel felt welcome in this gathering, yet apart. She viewed the room and its occupants like a painting, at a distance. Already everyone had divided into conversation groups. Tony, Julie, Pamela, and John, and Sam in a corner with Vittorio, their conversation punctuated with hands moving up and down, in and out, in an agitated manner.

"The price is getting harder to refuse, and with my cash-flow problem..." she heard Sam explain.

"They know better than to ask me." Vittorio's voice bordered on anger. "Maybe we can work something out that would be beneficial to both of us." The conversation continued quietly.

Emidio interrupted, "Enough of this shop talk. This is Thanksgiving."

"Right you are, Emidio," Sam said, smiling and putting his arms around his shoulders, "but we get together so seldom, old friend."

Angie announced that dinner was ready. After helping with platters of antipasto, Laurel found herself seated next to Vittorio. He was looking down the long table, and she wondered what he was thinking.

The implications of the conversation were of a merger of the Calomenis and the Bellinis. Was he planning to buy them out? She noticed his gaze light on Julie and Tony. Was their interest in each other as obvious to him as it was to her?

Pam seemed to hang on every word that John was uttering. She had the ability to make any man feel important. Angie had explained that Pam was a "poor little rich girl," largely left to her own resources by her family, and Laurel was better able to understand her need for one-upmanship. Pam's parents were now on one of their many cruises. Laurel was grateful her childhood had been constantly nourished by a loving family.

Vittorio tapped his glass with his spoon, and all eyes were upon him as he raised his glass to give a toast.

"This is in the form of a grace as well as a

toast. A Thanksgiving for Mama, Papa, Elise, Margaret and the way they touched our lives, and to family, friendship, and the future."

With this he raised his glass and tapped hers. So it went around the table, the sound of glass touching glass, all joining in the sentiment. Dinner had formally begun.

They were at the table most of the day, the many courses—pasta, fish, meat, vegetables, and the turkey—interrupted by lots of conversation, reflections on the harvest, memories of past Thanksgivings, so much to absorb.

She didn't know quite how it happened, but she agreed to go to the races Saturday with John, Pam, Julie, and Tony. Vittorio would be racing, and the more she thought about it, the more qualms she had.

Every time she tried to place herself a distance from Vittorio, she was drawn into the circle of his influence even more. He seemed pleased when she said she would go with the others.

Laurel couldn't deny that she wanted to be with him, to know him better, but her feelings were constantly ambivalent. She relaxed a little when she remembered that she would be just part of a group. The group would act as a shelter—a shelter from what, she wondered. From her own feelings? From Vittorio's? What were Vittorio's true feelings? That question opened another whole myriad of confusions. She would just go and enjoy herself for the day. She admonished herself for making something so complex out of something so simple.

Laurel had offered to meet them at the track, but Tony insisted that she ride with him and Julie, so she was sort of scrunched up in the back of the Porsche with the picnic lunch. John and Pam followed in another car built for a twosome.

The rest of the group had at least some understanding of automobile racing, educated by Vittorio's interest.

"This kind of racing is safer than most," Tony explained. "Some of these vintage cars are worth three hundred and fifty thousand dollars, and they're irreplaceable, so the kind of aggression and risk-taking that invites disaster is usually avoided. Vittorio got a good buy on his Ferrari. Took him a while to fix it up, but it's worth a lot now. Every now and then he bangs it up."

"Then why does he do it?" Laurel asked.

"He loves to drive," Tony said, "and he believes automobiles were designed to be used. You figure him out."

She remembered that day they drove to the church. Vittorio had said that it was the "feel" of the car in motion. Yes, to Vittorio automobiles were not static museum pieces that one simply could admire. Vittorio was an active, dynamic personality, and so would be his toys.

"After lunch you'll see an actual race. First there's the warm-up."

Numbers of people had already preceded them to the track. She noticed that there were a significant number of impressive cars right there in the parking lot. She had never before seen so many sports cars gathered in one place. She walked with the others to what they called the paddock area. Drivers and their crews were busy at work, adjustments being made, the sound of the engines filling the air. The atmosphere was insistent, compelling.

She marveled at the gleaming metal, polished chromed jewels, each a piece of dynamic sculpture, and underneath each hood—power. She walked a little behind the others, holding back. She didn't know why, but she wasn't quite sure she wanted to see Vittorio in this setting. She only knew that she hoped Vittorio would be safe.

What do you say to a toreador before he faces the full? Laurel smiled to herself at her melodramatics. There she was, going full tilt with her imagination again. So what if they went one hundred fifty miles per hour? Hadn't Tony and Vittorio indicated it was quite safe? She shrugged her shoulders and followed in the direction of the others. Even from a distance she could see Vittorio standing proudly by his red racing Ferrari, chatting with Tony and the others.

He looked as she knew he would, the racing suit molded to his body, white with gold letters emblazoned on his chest—Vittorio Bellini, in no way diminished by his peers or their machines that accompanied them. He matched the setting, and Laurel felt suddenly confident. Holding her hand out to Vittorio, she said, "I wish you luck."

"Thank you, Laurel." He drew her to one side, temporarily out of view of the others now inspecting the car.

"For luck, a kiss would seal the wish." He pulled her close. "Enough to make me want to pull through the race and not so much that I'll forget about racing altogether," he teased.

Matching his mood, she countered, "Well, we certainly wouldn't want to risk that."

"It might almost be worth it."

"What would be worth what?" Pamela gave Vittorio a dazzling smile.

"We were just talking about revving up our engines," Vittorio stated. "At what point it becomes dangerous."

"You will be careful, Vittorio." Pamela's voice held genuine concern.

"I'm always careful. And although winning is important, how I win is more so." His words were directed to Laurel. "Rick is part of my challenge." He threw back his head and laughed his deep, infectious laugh, all of them joining him without really knowing why.

Wishing him luck, they left the paddock area and climbed a small slope that over-looked a one-hundred-eighty-degree turn, half the track, and the finish line. Midst ice plant and stubble of native grass, they put down a blanket and over it a checkered table-cloth.

"Chicken, potato salad, and champagne—this is what I like about the races best," Tony said. "I leave the actual activity to my more daring brother."

"I'm glad you don't race," Julie said.

"No gladder than I am." Tony laughed and put his arm around her.

"It does seem a bit unnecessary," Pam added. She opened a can of macadamia nuts and offered some to Tony.

"Not those again." Tony pulled his hand away. "You know Vittorio and I both hate them."

"I'm mad about them, just a macadamia addict, but only this brand." She pointed to the red flowered can." Straight from the is-lands," she boasted and appeared to be more concerned with her nuts than the race that was in full swing before her.

Even from the hillside, the noise was deaf-ening. At first Laurel had trouble spotting Vittorio's Ferrari. She followed the track with her binoculars until she spotted his ap-proach. He moved so fast that it was easier to watch without the glasses, and she relied on the others to tell her his position.

To identify who was ahead must take practice. Ten laps and no stops for gas, she was told, each lap about two and a half miles. At this rate it would soon be over.

Laurel spotted the red Ferrari slowing into the one-hundred-and-eighty-degree turn once again, this time almost riding the bumper of another car—a Lotus. "He's trying to get inside on the turn," Tony explained, "and take first."

Laurel saw him straighten out at the turn, tilted a bit sideways, and disappear again out of sight. She gasped.

Tony assured her, "He's okay. Just going into a drift."

Another car pulled into the pits, and three or four antlike people were crawling all over it in an effort to fix whatever was wrong. Again Vittorio rounded the bend, still hugging the Lotus. There was something about the movement that was hypnotic, and she watched for the Ferrari, now having established its rhythm, always hugging the Lotus on the turn.

"Isn't that dangerous?" Laurel asked.

"He knows what he's doing."

The smell of burned rubber joined sound, exphasizing that these toylike creatures were indeed real, and she waited for the sight of the red Ferrari again. A slower yellow car rounded the bend, followed closely by Vittorio and the Lotus, now side by side.

"Vittorio's making his move," Tony exclaimed. "My God!"

The yellow car was a mass of smoke and steam. She heard the sound of metal meeting metal. She saw the red Ferrari fly on its side, the green Lotus sail across the track. Yellow and red flags were appearing from everywhere, the other cars now appearing almost motionless. Vittorio's Ferrari was still on its side. Men were rushing to it. The driver of the Lotus was already out of his vehicle— and still no sign of Vittorio.

Where was he? Laurel's breath now came in slow gasps. She buried her face in her hands, no longer able to look at the wreckage.

Someone on the hill said, "Oil on the track— see it?"

Laurel waited what seemed to be an eternity. *He has to be all right.* She repeated the phrase in her mind. *He has to be all right.* She dug her hands into the soil, clung to it, staring at the track, and she saw a body being lifted out of the red car.

Tony said, "He's okay."

She picked up the glasses and looked. Vittorio was on his feet, a little shaken, but smiling.

"Blast him!" Laurel said under her breath, relief and rage combined.

Vittorio waved in their direction.

"He knows we sit up here," Pamela said. "Look at that clown."

How can he? Laurel thought.

It took quite a long while for the cars to be towed and the oil spill cleaned. The other cars maintained their positions on the track at a slow speed, waiting for the race to resume.

Laurel was no longer interested in the race. Now she only wanted to see Vittorio, to be certain he was all right, but she didn't want to be the first to suggest it. Already she feared that her feelings for him were too apparent.

The accident had only intensified how much she cared for him. She was angry at herself for loving such a madman and angrier still at Vittorio for placing himself in such jeopardy. Torn between running down the slope and throwing herself into his arms or walking in the opposite direction forever, she followed Tony and the others down to the paddock.

One of the mechanics pointed under the Ferrari, now up on blocks, and Vittorio rolled out from beneath the car, just his head visible. "She seems to be okay," he indicated and slid out and stood up. "I don't want to do that often." He smiled.

"I should hope not!" Laurel shouted in anger and frustration. She could feel the tears well up behind her eyes and tried to look in another direction.

"I'm sorry I frightened you." He was talking to all of them.

"Vittorio," Pam exclaimed, "whatever am I going to do with you?" She seemed to take possession with her words.

"I even frightened myself that time. But see—I'm fine. Two legs, two arms, two eyes." He performed some exercise movement while speaking. "See—all in perfect working order."

"Everything but your brain," Laurel muttered under her breath.

"What was that?"

"I think she was questioning your mind." Tony laughed. "We're heading back to the ranch now to get ready for tonight, now that we have something to celebrate. Are you coming right home?"

"In a few minutes," Vittorio answered.

"Then Laurel can go back with you. She looked something like a pretzel in the back of the Porsche coming over, and I have to drive Julie home too."

"Good idea," Vittorio agreed.

Laurel was left with no choice, it seemed. She certainly didn't want to be the extra wheel in Julie and Tony's plans.

Pam looked quickly at John and took his arm, and they walked off together, absorbed in conversation.

"I'll drive slowly," Vittorio promised, holding up one hand in a Boy Scout gesture. They looked at Julie and Tony as they left holding hands.

"Well, my little one—" Vittorio moved toward Laurel and wrapped his arms around her.

Her tears spilled over; she was trembling. He calmed her. "I'm glad to know you care."

"Of course I care," she answered. "I'm not a robot."

"I never thought you were, my little tiger." He just held her closely until she felt comforted and reassured that all was right with the world, their world, at least for now.

Driving back to the ranch, Vittorio seemed to inch along, a contrast to his usual fast-forward style, and Laurel relaxed.

Vittorio reached across the gap between the seats and held her hand. Even the touch of his fingertips sent her messages of love. In that instant of almost losing him, her feelings had reached a crescendo, and she could feel herself tumbling down the scale, deep into a love for him that couldn't be denied.

No words were spoken between them on the long ride back to the ranch. She was glad for the silence. She didn't want this love— now. She wasn't ready, especially with Vittorio—stubborn, daredevil, her employer, she listed the reasons mentally that should bring her to her senses. Simultaneously she felt his touch, which seemed to erase all reason.

He stopped the car in front of the cottage

and, still with his hand in hers, bent over and kissed her.

"I'll pick you up at seven."

"Vittorio, I think—" She struggled to explain herself. "I think we—"

"Laurel." He drew her to him once again, his voice just a whispered warm breath in her ear. "Maybe it would be better if you just stopped thinking."

CHAPTER EIGHT

Laurel repeated his words, "Maybe it would be better if you just stopped thinking." Certainly her emotions were more than she could grasp intellectually. At that moment she was grateful to suspend thinking. The ordinary tasks that she must perform before seven would kill time until she saw Vittorio again. Lately her life seemed to be a series of small happenings that simply filled the time between her moments with Vittorio.

Plans were to go to the inn that evening, and from what Laurel had heard, the inn had an elegant atmosphere. Mooch seemed to chastise her for being absent all day by being underfoot, until she banished him to the front porch.

Selecting a jet-black V-neck dress, she pinned her hair back into a French twist that wisped out into soft curls at the nape of her neck. She was ready and waiting a full fifteen minutes before Vittorio was due.

Even Vittorio's knock was assertive. She opened the door.

"Stunning," he said. "You look stunning!"

Laurel accepted the compliment, looking down, away from those dark eyes that were admiring her without reservation. "Thank you."

"We'll meet the others there." He opened the car door for her, and with this small gesture she felt cared for.

The inn's soft pink outline could be seen ahead. They stopped in a circular drive at the entrance. Attendants took over from there, and they found themselves in an immense lobby with ceilings two stories high, supported by huge driftwood-colored beams, all contrasted by a wine terra-cotta floor. Surrounding a huge fireplace were oversized chairs and sofas upholstered in camel, with pillow accents of blue.

Behind them they heard John's voice. "Where are the kids?"

"You mean, Julie and Tony?" Vittorio asked. "They're coming."

"Why don't we have a drink while we're waiting?" John suggested.

He tucked Pamela's arm under his in such a way that it seemed to Laurel to establish them as a twosome. She looked at Vittorio to see his response. He was smiling and followed suit, taking her arm in his.

Seated, they ordered, and Laurel requested her favorite, a margarita.

"I don't know how you can stand all that salt," Pam exclaimed.

"It's the salt I like," Laurel said. She sipped the drink slowly, wondering what could be keeping the others.

After a half hour, Vittorio looked annoyed, suggested they go into the dining room, and left word with the maitre d' for Tony and Julie.

Laurel loved the dining room, a room within a room. Warm rose stucco walls were built inside wooden ones, and deep arched windows intensified a Mediterranean feeling.

Laurel was a bit awed by the prices and selections on the ample menu. Just as they were about to order, a flushed and excited Tony and Julie appeared on the scene, profuse with apologies.

"We're sorry we're late"—Tony hesitated— "but we were doing something important. We were getting engaged."

Julie thrust out her hand, where a substantial-looking diamond now rested, and they both anxiously looked at Vittorio for his response.

"It's about time Tony got off his duff!" Vittorio hugged his brother and Julie. "He's been mooning over Julie for years."

Laurel could see that Vittorio was genuinely pleased about the engagement. Her doubts as to Vittorio's loyalty were gradually being dispelled. His interest in her had been established and was evidently sincere. This put the whole matter in another light, an even more serious light.

Whenever Vittorio looked at her, he seemed to be studying her. His scrutiny was both uncomfortable and compelling. She tried to get involved with her dinner, knew it was delicious, but found it difficult to concentrate on how it tasted.

John proposed a toast to the engaged couple, and Julie offered another in thanksgiving for Vittorio's safety. Then Vittorio raised his glass. "To the Calomenis and the Bellinis, together in strength."

They drank the toast. "I hope we can hold out," John stated, "but in all honesty, Vittorio, is it practical?"

"It's not a question of practicality, John. It's a matter of principle. Little by little outside interests are controlling California land and its wine."

"We all can't afford the luxury of your principles, Vittorio," John countered.

Vittorio looked grim. "I have your father's promise, John." He spoke quietly. "He has promised to wait until I'm in a position to buy him out."

"My father's an idealist, and remember, Mother's half of the property was willed to Julie and me."

"And, Julie, how do you feel?" Vittorio asked.

Julie looked flustered. "This is the first I've heard about a sale. I'll have to talk to Father and then make my decision." She looked at Tony for help.

"Nothing can be settled tonight, Vittorio," Tony reasoned, "and you're putting Julie in the position of taking sides."

"As your wife, whose side will she be on?" Vittorio sounded angry now.

"Vittorio!" Laurel hoped he would stop and not spoil the evening for Tony and Julie. Things were already far too tense, and Tony was right—nothing could be resolved now.

No one in the party spoke for a few seconds. It was Pamela who broke the tension. "I won't have my evening spoiled by two hot-headed Italians or their wine." She looked at John, who couldn't help but laugh.

John extended his hand to Vittorio. "A truce. I hope it works out for you."

"A temporary truce." Vittorio took the outstretched hand.

Over dessert, the subject of wine was dropped and replaced by small talk about the wedding date. Laurel's attention was divided by the sounds of a flute softly playing during dinner. She excused herself on the pretext of going to the powder room, but with a resolve to find the musician. She hadn't told Vittorio her plans for music at the festival. This was her chance to hire someone truly accomplished, the only detail left in her plans.

The musician was unobtrusively tucked in

a corner of the massive room and seemed delighted to give Laurel his card so he could be contacted. Continuing on her journey to the powder room, she returned to the table, only to find the other couples had left.

Vittorio was alone, a bottle of iced champagne beside him. "They had to leave—out to spread the engagement news. They asked me to extend their good-byes."

Sitting beside him, Laurel sipped the champagne while the lyric sounds of the flute seemed to wrap them both in a soothing, protective cover, isolated from the rest of the world. Just the two of them alone, unconscious of others, "cocooned."

"It's been a good day," Vittorio murmured.

"How can you say that, Vittorio, when you almost ended it all on the track today?"

"Almost—that's the key word. We can't always protect ourselves, insulate ourselves, not if we want to live this life and not just sleepwalk through it. Do you understand?"

"I'm trying to," she whispered.

"Come." He took her hand, and they went out to the car.

He drove and parked on the winery property, at the top of a gradual slope, high enough so they could view row upon row of vines. They strolled hand in hand down the narrow gravel road.

"I want you to understand how I feel about this land."

"I'm trying to, Vittorio."

"It seems inevitable and realistic to surmise that large corporations of foreign interests eventually are going to control must of California's wine making. I know that's a realistic assumption. I don't deal in illusions, Laurel. Some might even say that it's already happened. But I think it's also realistic to think that Bellini Brothers can compete and that someday my children will continue with my work right here, as their great-grandfather did."

"How do you intend to succeed where others have failed?"

"Well, we're large enough, and with the Calomeni acquisition and the introduction of some jug wines.... I plan to be better than the competition. Advertising will be more important too."

"Suppose you can't acquire Calomeni's."

"But I will," he said. "I have other resources I can liquidate to do it, but I'll be taking a high risk. I'll gamble on our integrity and superiority." He said it without hesitation, as if it were finalized, as if it had already happened. "What are you thinking, Laurel?"

"You sound so confident."

"I must make a decision, and I have."

"And how will Tony feel?"

"I hope he'll go along."

"And if he doesn't?"

"One step at a time, Laurel."

They came to a point at the end of the road.

The moon sprinkled light on the landscape, creating a backdrop for the continuous line of small, bushy dwarfs that hugged the slope. Still holding Laurel's hand, Vittorio took her other hand and turned her toward him. Arms outstretched, he held her away, as if studying her. "Are you a gambler, my little tiger?" he asked.

She looked out over the fields, not wanting to meet his challenge. "No," she admitted.

"I know." He looked thoughtful, dropped her hand, and turned back in the direction of the car. Laurel was puzzled. He had made no demands on her, and she felt empty inside. She told herself that she didn't want his advances, which put her mind on neutral and sent her body in high gear. And yet to be completely set adrift made her feel wanting. Was this his new technique, to make her realize what she was missing, or had he lost interest?

He walked with her to the front porch of the cottage. "Thank you for listening."

"Thank you, Vittorio, for a wonderful evening."

He bent to her upturned face. His hands remained at his side, not holding her or touching her. He kissed her right temple and her left, the bridge of her nose, and then her mouth. She heard herself sigh as he turned and hurried down the steps.

The next morning a rose appeared, as if by magic, a lovely, single red rose, stuck in a wine bottle with a note attached to its stem:

Jogging tonight, 5:00. Yes? Of course, yes. Dinner tonight? Yes? Of course, yes.
                                        V.

He knew her too well, she thought. Of course, yes.

Laurel was on call all day for the deliveries for the festival. The round tables, linens, and chairs arrived before Pamela and her pictures and macadamia nuts.

Watching Pam munch away all day on the nuts, Laurel wondered with envy how she managed to keep that glorious figure. Once there, Pam did do her share. She and Laurel carried what seemed like hundreds of framed paintings into the reception room, and they were exquisite. With the aid of a ladder and one of the men from the cellars, they started with the hanging.

"A little to the left, lower, lower still," and so it went on into the day, with about half the job accomplished. They sat down on a couple of folding chairs and admired their work.

"Do you think that portrait is too close to the still life?" Pam asked.

"It's perfect," Laurel assured her. "Perfect."

"You're sure?"

"Not only am I sure, but I'm not moving from this chair for at least five minutes, even if they all fall off the wall."

"John helped me pick them out. You know, he's very knowledgeable about art."

"Are you dating John?"

"Some." Pam looked thoughtful. "A change of pace. You know, Laurel, Vittorio and I have been friends for a long time."

It was stated as an announcement, and Laurel wondered again if Vittorio's pursuit of her was just a change of pace.

Promptly at five, Vittorio appeared at her doorstep, dressed as she had seen him that first day when she was jogging. She bent over to adjust the ties on her running shoes. "How did you know I could make it?"

"I'm a gambler, remember. I thought the odds were with me."

"Are you always so sure of yourself?"

"Not always," he admitted. "Only when I bet on a sure thing."

"Such conceit." She looked at him with a steady gaze, his masculine good looks submerging her. "Oh, Vittorio." It was almost a defeated moan.

His next words were slow and deliberate. "You set the pace."

"The pace must be slow," she replied.

"Does he always come with you?" Vittorio referred to Mooch, already at their heels.

"Yes, he's my protector."

Vittorio laughed, that deep, throaty laugh that echoed in her dreams.

Every now and then Mooch would dash off

in some unknown direction and then return to join them. Breath for breath, Vittorio and hers, in and out, rhythmic, side by side— their movements sensual in synchronization. At the top of the hill she was breathless and relieved to be running on level ground for a while. As he leaned into a curve, Vittorio's arm lightly brushed hers, and she felt a surge of energy and moved ahead on the downhill stretch.

"Race?" he said, laughing.

Even with her advantage, he soon passed her by, waiting for her at the bottom of the hill, arms outstretched. Hurrying to catch up with him, she willingly collapsed in his arms.

This time he pulled away. "Dinner tonight?"

"Yes, of course, yes," she replied.

Getting ready for dinner, Laurel felt stupid. No wonder Vittorio didn't understand her. Every time she was with him, she sent him confusing signals of want and rejection. She would have to explain it to him tonight —that is, if she could first explain it to herself. She wasn't certain what he wanted from her. And what did he really know about her?

You trust people, and then they aren't there anymore—her father, then Rick.... She knew those feelings were irrational, and maybe with Vittorio it would be different. Certainly the intensity of her feelings for him far outstripped anything she had ever experienced before, and it was precisely that difference that frightened her.

Vittorio took her to a small café on the town square. Through leaded-glass windows Laurel could see there were only a few tables in the tiny restaurant. He held the massive oak door, and she felt that she had stepped back in time. The walls were papered in a small print, and round tables were covered in white linen, with sprigs of informal flowers in crystal bud vases. The planes of Vittorio's face appeared chiseled by the soft candlelight and shadow.

Laurel fingered her napkin, twisting it in her lap, wondering how to begin. She had to explain, to make it clear she was not playing games with him.

"Vittorio, I have to talk to you." That was the way she had rehearsed it.

"Yes?"

She should just try to say it like it was without putting him on the spot. "I think you're attracted to me, and I'm attracted to you, but I don't think I'm ready to— Well, I'm trying to make myself clear."

"That's supposed to be clear, my little tiger?"

"Vittorio, this isn't funny."

"It certainly isn't," he said.

"What I mean is, you're my boss, and I have no place for a relationship in my life right now. In other words, I don't know if we should be seeing each other."

"Do you want me not to see you anymore?"

She couldn't bear the thought of not seeing him again. She whispered, "No."

"Then what's the problem?"

"You're the problem, or I'm the problem. Oh, I don't know how to make you understand!" She was close to tears.

Vittorio reached across the table and closed his hand over hers. "We have time."

She was reassured. Yes, time. She didn't have to decide anything today. "Time," she said, relaxing. If he was willing to give her time, it must mean that he cared for her. "Thank you, Vittorio."

"You're quite welcome." He smiled. "I think the next order of business should be eating."

All of a sudden Laurel's appetite changed. She was ravenous. She ordered the soup, salad, rack of lamb, and her weakness, chocolate mousse. She was scraping the sides of the mousse dish with her spoon, licking the edges.

"Should I order you another?" He looked amused.

"No." She laughed. "I wasn't at all hungry when I came in here. I was so nervous."

"I don't know if I can afford to have you relax."

* * *

Vittorio drove slowly to the cottage, and Laurel invited him in for a cup of coffee. Going up the cottage walk, arm in arm, she noticed a light was on. She opened the door and saw a large figure on the couch. Laurel screamed. Vittorio moved, pulling the sleeping figure up by his shirt collar.

"Laurel, it's me—Rick!" the voice cried.

"Rick!" She stared in disbelief. "It's all right, Vittorio."

Vittorio dropped the somewhat unsteady figure, who fell back on the sofa in a sitting position.

Laurel was so shocked by Rick's presence, she was at a loss as to what to say. "Rick Webster, I'd like you to meet Vittorio Bellini."

"The guy who owns this place?" Rick extended his hand. "Pleased to meet you, sir."

"Do you always let yourself in unannounced?" Vittorio's voice was anything but friendly.

"Well, Laurel and I go a long way back." Rick went up to Laurel and put his arm around her, smiling, using his old, easy charm. She tried to pull away.

"I see." Vittorio's voice was controlled and dry.

He didn't see at all, Laurel thought, and before she could open her mouth to deny what he was thinking, he was turning to leave.

She broke away from Rick and followed him on the porch. "Vittorio, I'm sorry."

"Sorry for what?"

"About—about the coffee," she stammered.

"Quite all right," he muttered under his breath.

"You don't understand."

"I understand," he said quietly, "that I'm a fool."

CHAPTER NINE

"What are you doing here in my house without even telling me you were coming?" Laurel was furious at Rick. "And how did you get in?"

"The lady up at the house told me this was yours, and I climbed in the window. You ought to be more careful. I thought you might be glad to see me. After all—"

"After all what, Rick? You made it plain to me months ago, and frankly, I think you did me a favor."

"Laurel, I came to admit that I made a mistake. I explained in my letter."

Laurel had forgotten about the darn letter. Her voice softened. "I just wish you'd leave."

Rick looked astonished. "Can't we just discuss this whole thing a little more rationally? You owe me another chance, Laurel."

"I owe you nothing, Rick." Seeing him made it even more plain to her. They had dated in college—habit and convenience, nothing more. She wondered why she hadn't seen that then. "What we had was a college romance that we both have outgrown. My only regret is the way you broke up with me, not the breakup."

"I'm sorry, Laurel. That's why I'm here."

"It's too late, Rick, but I'm glad for your apology."

"Is there someone else?"

Laurel didn't answer. She didn't trust herself to answer. The issue with Vittorio was completely separate—no relationship to what she had felt for Rick. "Rick, you know what I say is true."

"Are you sure?"

"Yes."

"You mean it?"

"Yes," she said sadly.

He looked at her thoughtfully a moment. "Well, I always knew better than to beat my head against a stone wall." He said it good-naturedly, regretfully, with a shrug to his shoulder, as if resigned. "Friends?"

Laurel took a deep breath, "Friends," she replied. She made him a cup of coffee, and he didn't push to stay. Relieved, she watched him drive away until he was out of sight.

Too late, Mooch appeared on the porch, somewhat breathless from an evening run. "Darn you, Mooch! Where were you when I needed you? You're supposed to guard the place."

Rick couldn't have picked a worse moment to try to enter her life again. Same old Rick —laid-back and casual. She compared him with Vittorio's substance—nothing casual there, she thought. Vittorio could do with a bit of casual.

Of course, he had read more into the situation than was true. Rick's performance hadn't helped. Should she try to explain, or wait for Vittorio to think it over? If she really meant something to him, surely he— But he was such a proud man. Back and forth, Laurel pondered her dilemma while busy with the festival preparations and monitoring the wines. Running away looked good to her again.

The pruners were attacking the fields now—slow, tedious work by skilled hands. They moved up the rows, attending to each individual vine, instinctively knowing where to cut to ensure the quantity and quality of next year's harvest. She caught a glimpse of Vittorio among them, his bent-over form distinctive to her even from a distance.

She remembered that first day she'd seen him, how she had thought he was a field hand. Yes, the description suited him. In spite of his sophistication, his powerful shoulders and sturdy build conformed to the land. Tony was right. Vittorio belonged here. As Tony had said it, "Married to the wine."

* * *

Weeks of organization were paying off. The reception room was all she had imagined. Tony assured her the invitations had been mailed on time, and the brochures featuring the new wine were finished. Already the festival had been covered in the San Francisco newspaper wine columns. By giving the new wine so much attention, much of the Bellinis' reputation was focused on this event. Laurel was beginning to have second thoughts about the festival. Too much that was important to Vittorio hinged on its success.

Emidio, too, had his doubts. "This is no way to go about it," he said, "all this commotion over the release of one new wine."

"Is it a good one?" she asked.

"Yes, the best white blend we've ever produced, but have you seen Vittorio lately? He's in a mood. I've never seen him like this. This is a winery, not a coming-out party," he muttered. "Maybe something else is bothering him. Do you know what's gotten into him? Look at him, out in the fields exhausting himself." He looked at Laurel, waiting for a response.

"I haven't seen him lately," was all she said.

"Well, you're lucky," Emidio grumbled.

Laurel hadn't seen Vittorio except out in the fields, and at night she lay in bed listening for the throb of his Ferrari's engine. He was out every night and didn't return until the wee hours of the morning. Laurel wondered where—with Pamela?

Vittorio seemed to have ignored the festival preparations. She would have appreciated his input, but she found out from the other workers that he had poked his head in from time to time. She guessed he must be satisfied, because she hadn't heard from him.

On the Saturday of the festival it looked like rain. Rain would be welcomed by the dry valley but not that day. She hoped for one more sunny day, so guests could spread out on the terrace and enjoy the magnificent view. *Good wine can only be better when the atmosphere is right*, she thought, and she had worked hard to create a warm yet elegant occasion.

Guests began arriving at the prescribed hour of one, and the wine tasting and partying began. Vittorio circulated among the crowd.

"What a splendid idea!" one gentleman said, stopping him.

"Our way of saying thank you from the Bellinis." Vittorio answered, then threaded his way through the gathering, greeting individuals here and there. He was heading straight for Laurel.

He gave her a warm smile, as if nothing had happened between them, but his eyes didn't reflect the smile. He held her arm tightly, too tightly. "You've done a magnificent job, but I knew you would." There was no expression in the words.

She had decided to explain to him about the evening with Rick, but not now in the middle of all this commotion. This certainly wasn't the time.

The sound of the flute playing in the background caused Vittorio to pause a moment, and he released her. She slipped into the crowd. He looked about, startled, but Emidio was summoning him from across the room, and Vittorio joined him at the microphone.

"My friends, you've sampled many of our wines, but we'd like to introduce a new wine on the market."

The servers were standing on the sidelines with the bottles, labels covered by their hands. Even Laurel hadn't seen the name of the wine. Glasses on trays were being passed to the waiting group. It was a dramatic moment, and Vittorio took the opener and removed the cork.

"To Mama and Papa," he said solemnly and announced the name of the wine—"Heritage." Everyone clapped, and the wine flowed. Laurel floated through the crowd, trying to get a feel for the response.

"Superb. What's the wholesale on it?"

"Excellent. Did you hear he sold his shirt, wants to buy out the Calomenis?"

"His brother's marrying the daughter— shouldn't hurt his chances."

"I thought Vitto was set up to marry her."

"You know Vitto—he's not the marrying kind."

"He doesn't have to," was the laughing reply.

"Maybe Pam will snag him yet."

Laurel didn't linger to hear the rest of the conversation, but it smarted just the same. Suddenly she felt as if she were involved in a cat-and-mouse game and that she was the mouse. Maybe Rick had done her a favor by appearing on the scene. Perhaps Vittorio considered a conquest worth fighting for simply because it was denied him. Apparently he wasn't used to being refused. She wondered how she had become so involved, how she could be so clearly in love with someone whose motivations she suspected. It just didn't make much sense.

She checked in the kitchen to see how things were coming along, but when Vitto walked back into the room, the whole atmosphere had changed. Previously, a feeling of good will had prevailed, and now she could sense a restlessness. People were rushing to the windows, and on the horizon, at the rim of the valley, there was an enormous cloud that changed from charcoal to black, red, and gold. It could mean only one thing. Fire!

Vittorio announced over the microphone, "We've been asked to evacuate, just as a precaution, from the existing fire." His voice sounded assured and calm. "We've been informed by the authorities that there's no reason to panic. If you would just leave in an orderly fashion and head out of the valley south in the direction of San Francisco, our staff will direct your departure."

The crowd started to rush toward the doors. "I emphasize"—Vittorio's voice was arresting—"there is no need to panic."

The guests seemed to respond, but even so, Laurel was swept by the tide of people who were heading toward the exits.

Already the air was pungent with the smell of smoke, and yet it seemed so far away. She tried to walk against the crowd but couldn't seem to gain ground. She wanted to get to Vittorio, to find out what she could do to help. She knew what fire could mean to the vines, to the winery.

She couldn't see above those who were exiting. "Excuse me—excuse me." She tried to worm her way in the opposite direction, when she felt a hand on hers, a strong hand—his —that pulled her, and soon she was enveloped in his embrace, tucked under his arm, protected and drawn to the edge of the room.

"This is serious," Vittorio said. "The wind isn't helping. There'll be an emergency shelter at the church. You'll be needed there, and take Emidio with you. I sent him to the cottage."

"I want to stay and help."

"You're to go to the church. I don't have time to argue with you, Laurel. Sprinklers are already on in the fields. The cellars are

sealed. Julie and Pam have already left."
And at her protest, he shouted, "Just get out
of here, will you? Don't you have enough
sense to know when you're in the way?" He
left her standing there.

She exited through the kitchen. Emidio
was waiting on the cottage porch.

"I'm staying," the elderly man stated
firmly.

"No, Emidio. We have to go," Laurel told
him, with Vittorio's angry words still vivid in
her mind. "Vittorio says he has things under
control, and we'll be needed at the church."

She called for Mooch, circled the small
building, and called again. She ran franti-
cally across the road and yelled, but he didn't
come. "I can't leave without him."

This time it was Emidio who spoke with
authority. "Dogs have an instinct. He'll be all
right. Vittorio is right—this is no place to be
right now. Look!"

Laurel's eyes were already beginning to
sting. The sky at the ridge of the property
was completely shrouded in black. Flames
were shooting some one hundred feet in the
air. Laurel had never seen anything like it,
and she was frightened. Watching as that
natural force was unleashed, an overwhelming feeling of helplessness seized her.

As if sensing her feelings, Emidio took her
hand. "Come, Laurel. All we can do is pray
for a change in the wind." He hesitated when
they got to the car.

"I won't go without you," she said. Obediently he joined her, and they drove away, leaving the mass of flames that threatened the Bellini Brothers Winery and the surrounding countryside.

Heading south toward the church, they found progress was slow on the country road. People were standing by the side, eyes locked to the blackened sky that was threatening to take their homes.

Things were in motion at the church. The recreation hall was set up with cots. Two doctors had volunteered for first aid, and the Red Cross was setting up a kitchen. Laurel pitched in, making beds, helping to carry in supplies.

Valiant and heartbreaking stories accompanied the people who sought refuge at the church, those who battled the fires with buckets and hoses, only to see their homes go up in flame.

Firefighters were called from as far away as Monterey. Bulldozers, aircraft, and helicopters were being brought in to help, but the fire continued on into the night and was still not contained the next day, and everyone's concern increased.

The collection of stunned, displaced people who came in and out of the church for food and rest brought home to Laurel how fire had the power to destroy men's dreams. Pam and Julie passed her in their routine tasks and wore the same worried, fatigued expression that Laurel knew matched hers. Emidio paced the room like a caged animal.

In that setting Pam worked shoulder to shoulder with the rest of the crew, dropping her pretensions. Laurel reluctantly admitted to herself that Pam was likable and helpful. Maybe that was the side of Pam that Vittorio saw. A nice and beautiful Pam seemed even more threatening. Could whatever Vittorio felt for Pam still be smoldering to spark again, just as the live coals in this devastating fire? Was his interest in her sincere? Laurel chided herself for asking these questions. After their last parting, it didn't seem to matter.

There had been no word from Vittorio, Tony, or the Calomenis. Julie was particularly concerned for her father, who would not leave. "He's not that well," she explained.

The wind pattern was changing, and, according to officials, the fire pattern was becoming controlled, the worst over. That night Laurel lay on one of the cots in an effort to catch some sleep. Almost at the point of sleep, she felt someone nudge her. Julie said, "Listen."

Soon everyone in the room was cheering. Rain, blessed rain, was gently tapping the roof. Julie and Laurel exchanged glances; it wasn't over yet.

The next day people without homes were being offered temporary sanctuary by those more fortunate in the area. The church facility was closed down.

Laurel's one thought was to get back to the winery. She was filled with apprehension about Vittorio's welfare, and also about Mooch's. The little dog had become family to her, her only family in California. All this confusion would certainly bewilder him, and he might lose his ability to find his way home. The Humane Society had picked up hundreds of animals—dogs, cats, goats, cows —and relocated them. She wondered if Mooch could be part of that group. How would she even begin to track him down?

Julie had left for the Calomenis' by the time Laurel and Emidio climbed into her car. When they reached the main road, the full realization of what had happened in the last few days took hold. In many places the road was a dividing line between the decimated and the undecimated. Some homes, by some quirk of fate, had been spared, and others had burned totally to the ground, just a chimney marking the spot where once families had conducted their lives.

Laurel wondered how people could recover from such loss. The immensity of the fire's power was beginning to take hold, and she started to tremble, anxious for the safety of Vittorio, Tony, and Mooch—afraid of what she might find.

Emidio seemed numb, riding in silence beside her. "I'm certain that Vittorio and Tony are fine," he said, as if to comfort them both. "They aren't foolish men."

The closer they got to the Bellini ranch, the more alarmed they became. Several acres of vineyards had been wiped out, but they became more positive when they saw the fire line had broken before they turned the bend approaching the Bellinis' road. The house was standing, as were the cellars, and the immediately surrounding land remained untouched. They could see where the fire had seared a pattern to the edge of the wide gravel road that circled the property. Vittorio and Tony had been lucky to lose just the acreage to the south.

"The wind must have been with us," Emidio said with a sigh of relief.

"The wind and God," Laurel said softly.

In spite of Emidio's strong protest, she dropped him off with instructions to rest.

"You won't be any help to any of us if you're ill." She spoke sharply and immediately regretted being so irritable. "I'll let you know as soon as I know anything."

There was no sign of life at the big house, not any at the cellars. Everyone must still be fire watching. Vittorio must be all right. There were no reports of deaths, she assured herself, and most injuries had first come to the church. Of course, he was all right. Nothing could harm that crazy Italian. Then why wasn't he back? *Calm down*, she cautioned herself. *No one else is back, either. You're worrying needlessly.*

Approaching the cottage, she hoped to see the familiar wag and round, eager form of Mooch on the porch, but there was no sight of him. She walked across the gravel road and called, walked the whole length of the property, shouting his name until her voice was raw, until she reached the edge across which she could only see the flat emptiness that the fire had left there.

"Oh, dear Mooch, do you think that I've abandoned you?" she whispered aloud.

She must have been searching for Mooch an hour. Turning back, she saw a light in the kitchen of the main house, and she ran down the road. Bursting through the door, she saw Angie sitting there as if nothing had happened, sipping a mug of coffee.

"You look disappointed," Angie commented.

"Oh, no, it's just that I've been looking for Mooch. I'm so glad you're back and that everything is all right."

"Vittorio insisted that I go immediately to my sister's. He had one of the men drive me."

"There's no one up there." Laurel pointed to the top of the property. "Where are they?"

"Exhausted, probably," Angie said. "Tony came by a few minutes ago to say he was going to check on Julie."

"Had he seen Vittorio?"

"Yes, he's fine. He's gone to get the Ferrari

and to take Pam home—she's stuck at the Calomenis'. He had someone park the Ferrari on the other side of the road."

So he was fine, hadn't even bothered to check on her whereabouts, had instead gone to Pamela and his precious Ferrari. Well, that certainly told Laurel where she stood!

Maybe he had stopped while she was out looking for Mooch. She consoled herself with the possibility, taking the cup of hot coffee offered by Angie, looking anxiously out the window. Maybe it would be better if she wasn't here when he got back. After all, the fire may have wiped out everything in sight, but it hadn't removed the ugliness of their last encounter. Theirs was a bond of mutual distrust, hardly the stuff to build a permanent relationship on. He had said he was a fool, no more than she.

"I'm going now, Angie. I'm exhausted."

"No wonder. It's been a tiring two days for all of us."

"Thanks for the coffee."

"Sleep well in spite of it."

"No problem, if only I could find Mooch."

"If he comes here, I'll bring him right down, no matter what time it is. I'm sure he'll be back. He knows when he's latched on to a good thing."

"Tomorrow I'll check the Humane Society lists. They'll be posted at the church and run in the paper. Are the phones still out?"

"Probably be several days before they're

operational. We're lucky that's our only inconvenience."

"I promised to phone Emidio. He's so worried," Laurel said.

"I'll let him know," Angie said. "Go and take care of yourself now."

She left and ran down the steps, calling Mooch as she went.

Later, in bed, she listened for the familiar sound of the Ferrari. Her thoughts churned with memories of Mooch and Vittorio—poor Mooch, who must think he was forgotten; Vittorio and their misunderstandings.

Images of Vittorio kept coming to mind: Vittorio in the fields, bronzed and full of vitality, his broad shoulders bent to a task; Vittorio jogging beside her; Vittorio, his almond eyes outlined by candlelight; Vittorio's hand, his strong fingers touching hers; Vittorio, buried by his car on the track; Vittorio with Pamela on his arm. Laurel shook her head, as if to erase the memory, and remembered instead his arms around her and the sensations they evoked.

The restlessness that seized her was painful and unrelenting, and then she heard the welcome sound of the Ferrari. It went up the road and didn't stop. *Just as well*, she thought, tears welling up in her eyes.

CHAPTER TEN

Laurel turned on her bedside light and noted the time, midnight. All this time to get the car and take Pamela home. She took a tissue and wiped her nose, the tears still flowing. It was just that she was so tired, she rationalized, the last few days having taken their toll. All she needed was sleep. One thing at a time. She switched off her light, put her face in her pillow, muffling the sobs that seemed to come in waves. She felt ridiculous acting this way when she had so much to be grateful for.

Hearing a sound on the porch and hoping for Mooch, she opened the door. A struggling Mooch was being balanced in the powerful arms of what appeared to be Vittorio. They were a sorry pair, blackened by soot and smoke, and Vittorio looked as if he were on the verge of collapse.

"I brought you a present." He deposited

Mooch on the kitchen floor. "Do you know how many nondescript dogs were relocated during this fire?" He went to the sink and washed his hands and face. "I must have gone to two dozen houses before I found him. I almost gave up." He managed a weak smile, but his eyes looked hollow, and his voice cracked when he spoke. The lines around his eyes, still etched with soot, made him look much older, and he sat down on her bed.

"Oh, Vittorio!" was all she could say. She knelt at his feet. "How did you know?"

"I knew you left him behind. I watched to see that you'd leave, and when he wasn't here when I got back, I knew you'd be frantic. Besides, it's my way of an apology for the other night. I know I don't own you, Laurel, but when I saw the other guy, I—"

"I was as surprised as you were. Rick and I— Well, it's nothing. You never give me a chance to explain."

He cradled her head. "I know." He sounded dejected. "Tact isn't one of my strong points."

He glanced down at his dirty clothes and looked at the bedding, dismayed. "I shouldn't sit here. I wasn't thinking." He put his face in his hands.

"You're exhausted, Vittorio. It's all right. Everything is washable."

"Do you mind then?" He stretched out on the bed. "Just need to rest for a few minutes. My mistake was in slowing down. I was all right as long as I kept moving." He sank into the bedding, almost in collapse, closed his eyes, and in less than a minute she heard the rhythmic sound of his breathing.

She administered to Mooch, now licking her all over, and she was engulfed in sooty fur. He appeared to be all right except for his disheveled appearance. After a bowl of food and some water, he curled up in a corner of the kitchen and fell asleep.

Laurel looked at the huge sleeping form of Vittorio. The length and breath of him reduced her bed to less than half its size. He was a sleeping giant, and she sat in her small rocker, content just to watch him. His hair was tousled and framed his face. She could imagine him as a child, a sturdy little boy with loops of curls and a determined face. He didn't stir.

She curled up on the small sofa in the other room and listened to the rhythm of his breathing, which soon lulled her to sleep.

Awakening to the sound of the shower, Laurel was puzzled. Vittorio's visit had seemed almost a fantasy, but the activity in the shower, which led off the bedroom, made her well aware of the reality of Vittorio's presence in her house. His singing, above the level of the shower flow, filled the tiny cottage with sound.

Coming into the bedroom, wearing his sooty clothes, he planted a kiss on her forehead, like his being there was an everyday occurrence.

"Vittorio," she began.

"No speeches," he countered. "First break-fast. I'm famished, haven't eaten for twenty-four hours."

"Vittorio!" She sounded annoyed.

"Laurel," he said, looking at her steadily, "it's all right."

Laurel retreated into the bedroom to shower and change.

She didn't know quite how to handle Vittorio's buoyant behavior. It was just that they still had issues to settle. She loved him, she knew with certainty, but.... Why did she always deal in "buts"? What was wrong with her, anyway! She lathered her hair and soaked her head, letting the warm water run over her in an attempt to clarify her thoughts.

Stepping out of the shower, she could smell the aromas of hot coffee mingling with bacon, and she decided that she was famished too. Her wet hair turbaned in a towel, she slipped into a terry robe and padded her way into the kitchen where an exuberant Vittorio was busy being chef. She set the table and they sat opposite each other.

A question formed on Vittorio's lips and died there. "We'd better eat."

She couldn't help smiling at the way he attacked his food. "Are you certain that it's only been twenty-four hours?"

He paused long enough to say, "I want to take you somewhere special today."

"Today?"

"Right now."

"But—"

His look admonished her.

"All right," she said.

In twenty minutes she was seated beside him in the Ferrari headed for the coast. It was enough to be with him; for once she'd think only of now.

The car seemed to have memorized the winding back-country road, where sheep grazed on meadows, and bare-branched apple orchards rested up for their springtime awakening. They stopped in a small restaurant where the smells of homemade bread mingled with fresh-grounded coffee.

Following the Russian River down through redwood forests, they emerged to their first glimpse of the ocean, an endless horizon— flat, gray, blue, indigo, with flocks of white egrets feeding on bleak shores.

They passed Fort Ross and continued down the coast. Vittorio turned left on a narrow graveled road, somewhat secluded from view by wild, rambling berry vines and fallen logs. Laurel could see he was excited about their destination, as if he were anxious for her reaction. "This is my retreat," he said.

Passing between dense undergrowth, they came out on a clearing, a small peninsula that jutted out to the ocean. Set on the point of the triangular piece of land was a low-rise driftwood cabin that hugged the landscape.

The unobtrusive building rose from the materials that it sat on, grayed, weathered, fitting. "I've never brought anyone here before," Vittorio said.

Laurel felt privileged and grateful to be the first. He opened the door with a flourish, and she stepped inside to a window view of the cliffs below, waves pounding, the spray rising in a mist.

"You own this?" She was overwhelmed, as if anyone could own the universe, for that's what it seemed to her, a private world.

"Yes, do you like it?"

"I don't know how to say how much." Her eyes focused on the magnificent view.

"I purchased the property about five years ago and took some things from an old estate to furnish it." He crossed to the fireplace, a huge rock walk-in cavern, and lit the set fire.

Laurel looked around. He could be justly proud of what he'd done. The furnishings were a blend of brass, copper, and wood. She admired the beamed ceiling and ran her hand over the smooth wooden kitchen sideboard.

"I did the finishing work. This is where I come when all else fails me." He showed her the bedroom, dominated by an antique postered maple bed, lifting the mattress, indicating the rope substructure. "This is the way they used to do it."

She pressed on the uneven, puffy bedding.

"That's a feather bed," he explained, "for

resting and nesting. Rain, sleet, or snow. When you sink into that, you're warm."

"When I'm with you," she said, "warm is not my problem." She moved to distance herself from him.

On the wall was a woven hanging, variegated blues, magenta accents, and knobby whites that simulated clouds over an ocean setting. "I picked that up at a local gallery, but I made these." He indicated the bathroom mirrors framed with shells. "You like it?" He waited her assurance.

"Love it, love it." She hugged him. "Love it," and she brushed away a tear.

"Do you always cry when you're happy?"

"Only when I'm *very* happy," she said, laughing.

In the kitchen she opened all the cupboards one by one.

"I didn't know you were a snoop." He stretched out on a woolly rug in front of the fire, observing her.

"Just getting acquainted." She fixed them hot chocolate with a dash of brandy and joined him.

"Something to warm you up," she teased.

"You can snoop any time." He gave her a little kiss.

"No one has ever been here before?" she asked again.

"No one!"

She took the large mugs to the sink and washed them. She went to place them in the cupboard when a large can of macadamia nuts caught her eye, a can covered with bright red flowers—Pamela's special brand, a sharp reminder of something she'd almost forgotten. Macadamias—who else for but Pam? Laurel might be the first, but would she be the last? Her mind raced through a murky scenario.... Confusion gripped her. Where did she really stand?

"Laurel." She barely heard his voice. "Come over here," he called.

"I—I want to head back," she said.

He looked at her, shocked. "I want to talk to you about—"

"I'm not in the mood for conversation, Vittorio."

He tried to pull her close, and she pushed him away.

"Back to the winery, of course." His tone was harsh. "Thank God I have the winery. At least she follows her nature. At least she knows when to yield."

"Just because I want to go back—" she shouted at him. "You don't understand!"

"Don't you ever lead with your heart?"

"You're not being fair."

"Fair! You think you're fair?" His face was set in an expression of disdain. "Maybe you just aren't woman enough..."

She didn't hear the end of the sentence; it was as if he had slapped her. There were no more words. The trip back was filled with silence.

* * *

In the days that followed, Vittorio's words continued to mock Laurel. The sound of his Ferrari, coming and going, was enough of a reminder to disturb her dreams. She didn't know how much longer she could go on reliving the nightmare of their quarrel, what she knew was their final separation.

Thank heaven there were only a few days before her scheduled trip. Just to be removed from this intolerable situation for a few days was what she had been clinging to.

"You look like you'll be ready for a rest." Emidio looked concerned. "Is it my imagination, or have you been losing some weight? Perhaps we're working you too hard."

Even Laurel had noticed that her appearance had been left wanting of late, the hollows under her eyes evidence of her sleepless nights.

"And Vittorio looks no better," Emidio continued, "but no wonder—he's never home. Comes in at the crack of dawn, out every night, gone every weekend. I'm worried about him, Laurel. Something is eating at him. I know him like my own son. I must be candid with you. I've noticed how you've been avoiding each other. Can I help?"

"Thank you, Emidio." She went over to her friend and gave him a hug. "I'm afraid this situation is beyond anyone's help."

"Sometimes when you're too close to a situation, it's difficult to see the solution. His heart is good, Laurel."

Laurel looked away. "Thank you for trying."

The only solution that Laurel could see was for her to complete her contract and leave. The week before, she had sent out her résumé, but it was too soon for any bites. She hadn't mentioned it to Emidio. Why worry him until it was a certainty? Perhaps when she came back. Nothing would happen over the holidays, anyway.

Tony was at a loss without Julie, and he frequently stopped by Laurel's for a chat. He, too, noticed. "You're working too hard. This afternoon you're going on an expedition."

"Tony, I can't."

"I've cleared it with Emidio. There's a sidewalk arts-and-crafts show on the square, a good opportunity for Christmas shopping. How about it?"

Laurel had given little thought to Christmas, and she did need gifts to take home. "Maybe I do need a change."

"Then it's settled."

The complete square was surrounded with tables and easels. Laurel and Tony were soon caught up in selecting from the many attractive items for sale. There were regional oil paintings, leather-tooled belts and fine handbags, photographs, stained glass, macramé, needlecrafts, wooden toys and soapstone sculptures. She was impressed with the quality of the workmanship and equally pleased that many were within her budget.

"I think I can get all my shopping done right here," she said while purchasing leather belts for her stepfather and brother.

"Look at this," Tony called from the next table. He was on his hands and knees, operating a small wooden steam shovel that was exquisitely made. Every movement was doweled, and the feel of the wood was smooth and satiny.

"Are these for children?" she asked the vendor.

"Yes—and guaranteed to stand up to any abuse short of a jackhammer." The young man laughed. "There's a lot of work in them, but I designed them to last."

"Get a load of this sports car," Tony exclaimed.

"They're for big kids too," the man added.

"Vittorio would get a charge out of this," Tony said.

Yes, Laurel thought, he qualified—a big kid. Laurel purchased the steam shovel and road grader for her two nephews, and Tony bought the sports car.

"I don't know if I'll be able to part with this, but I know Vittorio would love it." And then as an aside, he added, "What's happened between you and Vittorio, Laurel? I thought that—"

"Whatever there was is over." Laurel could

feel that old, familiar lump rise in her throat again.

"I'm sorry." Tony put his arm about her shoulders and guided her to an ice-cream stand. "Two ice-cream cones," he said and handed her one.

They spent the rest of the afternoon browsing and buying. Tony bought Julie a small heart-shaped pendant.

"She'll love it," Laurel agreed.

A light rain began to fall. They ran toward the car, clutching their packages. "We might as well make it dinner too," Tony suggested. "How about some Mexican food for a rainy day?"

The drizzle had now turned to sheets of rain, good for the burned-out soil, she thought, and then she laughed at herself. She was almost as compulsive as Vittorio was about the winery.

"Why not?" she answered. "This is the best time I've had in weeks. Thank you, Tony. I think Julie is a very lucky girl."

"Then Mexican it is."

The Mexican restaurant was housed in what seemed at first a small adobe house that someone might find quite comfortable to live in, but the one-room entryway branched into several dimly lit dining rooms. Rough-hewn wooden tables, low ceilings, and tiled floors set the mood of authenticity. Tony and Laurel were directed to a secluded table in the corner of the room and handed a massive menu.

"That's the problem," Laurel remarked.

"What problem?"

"What to order." Laurel scanned the list and options. "Decisions, decisions."

"I've solved the problem." Tony pointed to the menu. "I always order this. I know I like it, and I don't want to take a chance on ordering something I'll hate. Not too adventurous, is it?" He sounded as if he were apologizing.

"Well, if you know you like something...." Laurel pondered over the menu. How different Tony was from his brother—careful, cautious, safe.

The waitress was standing beside them now with pencil and pad, looking at Laurel for direction.

I can't make the simplest decision, she thought, and she didn't know why, but she felt uncomfortable. "Take his first." She nodded at Tony.

He ordered. "The chili relleno, enchilada combination, and a small pitcher of sangria."

The waitress was still waiting, and Laurel had a feeling that whatever she decided would be the wrong decision. She felt inadequate and pointed to the menu.

"This—" Then, feeling embarrassed, she said to Tony, "You'd think this was a lifetime decision."

"Those are easy," Tony said. "It's these little ones that get you."

"I don't know what's wrong with me lately," she confessed. "I find any decision a big chore." She was thinking of Vittorio, his declaration of love. What if she just led with her heart as he'd suggested? She sipped the sangria and tried to relax. Anyway, that option was over now, severed by Vittorio's angry words. She bowed her head, and the tears came involuntarily to her eyes.

"What is it, Laurel?"

"I can't talk about it."

"Maybe I can help."

"I'm just fine, just fine." She blinked back the tears. "I guess I'm just tired, ready for a vacation." She managed to smile.

"Well, that's an improvement." Tony poured her another drink.

"Have you heard from Julie lately?" she asked.

"I call her every other day, and we write. These separations are driving me up the wall!"

Laurel laughed at his intensity. "I'm glad their place wasn't damaged by the fire."

"Me too. You know we're negotiating to buy them out." He looked thoughtful. "I wish Julie weren't involved with this."

"What do you mean?"

"I don't want the business part of this to interfere in our relationship. Although I have a financial interest in the winery, it's really

Vittorio's. Buying out Sam is his idea, his dream."

"I'm certain he'll be fair."

"Oh, sure," Tony answered. "And he can handle it, but suppose some outside interest outbids him? Sam would sell to Vittorio for sentimental reasons, but John? And that puts Julie on the spot because of her feelings for me. I don't want her caught in the middle, and I don't want to be there, either."

"I guess it could get awkward, but you're worrying about something that hasn't even happened yet," she tried to comfort him.

"True, but you know Vittorio. He always gets what he wants, and John can be almost as stubborn."

"Yes, I know Vittorio." Laurel sighed and reached across the table and put her hand on his. "Julie is lucky."

"You're absolutely right." And then more seriously, he said, "I'm the lucky one."

The waitress brought their dinner, warning, "Be careful, the plates are very hot."

Laurel followed the waitress's movements as she left the table, admiring her peasant costume. She caught a glimpse of someone standing in the archway.

Even in the dim light she recognized him. It was Vittorio, and Pamela was beside him. How long had they been standing there? Pam made a move in their direction, but Vittorio caught her arm. Tony had his back to the entrance.

"What's wrong?"

Laurel looked down at her plate. "It's just so much food."

"The only solution is to attack," he said.

Laurel stabbed her enchilada with her fork and cut it into two with one stroke, looked up again, and Vittorio was gone. She took a huge bite.

"'Attack' was just a figure of speech," Tony said.

Hot pepper burned Laurel's throat, and she swallowed some water, "Excuse me a minute." Getting up, she headed for the ladies' room, shaking all over. She needed to get hold of herself. If just the sight of Vittorio was able to affect her like this, she was thankful that her trip to Minnesota was only two days off. It hadn't taken him much time to seek refuge in Pam, she thought.

She leaned against the tile wall, staring at the floor, feeling ridiculous and childish. *So this is the independent Laurel Miller, hiding in the bathroom.* Suddenly the absurdity of the situation made her laugh out loud. She straightened her shoulders and ran a comb through her hair, applied lipstick, and bolted out the door—only to collide with the very person she was trying to avoid.

Vittorio seemed surprised too. "I was headed for the—" He indicated the adjacent door.

"Well, yes, I'm sorry," she said. "I wasn't looking where I was going."

"Did you have a good dinner?" he asked casually.

"Very nice, thank you."

"I understand you leave for Christmas in a couple of days."

"Yes."

"I hope you have a nice trip."

"Thank you. I hope you have a nice Christmas."

They were exchanging amenities as if they were strangers.

"Good of Tony to take care of the Bellini farewells."

"Yes, he's a good friend."

"You seem to have a knack for gentleman *friends*."

"And you, women! Give Pamela my best wishes for the holidays."

CHAPTER ELEVEN

Laurel crossed what seemed an endless plain to return to Tony.

"Cold Mexican food isn't the best." Tony looked at her plate.

"I can't finish it, anyway," she said.

"But you've hardly eaten."

"I think the ice cream is still with me," she apologized. "If you're done Tony, I'd like to head back. I've a lot to do in the next couple of days."

All was in order for her trip. Emidio was going to dog-sit Mooch, and Tony had offered to drive her to the airport. Laurel was thankful that Emidio had not questioned her about her uncharacteristically quiet behavior. She felt that she was betraying him by not telling him that she was leaving soon. She performed her duties at the winery almost mechanically. The day of departure, she left him a small Christmas package, a hand-tooled wallet purchased at the fair, and kissed him a fond farewell.

"Come back soon," he called, waving from the lab door.

Strapped in her seat in the airplane, Laurel looked out on the runway. *I wish I knew where my destiny lies*, she thought. It was a silent prayer, repeated as she closed her eyes, repeated in cadence to the steady sound of the engines. She slept for a short while before the stewardess brought refreshments.

Travel of any kind was a treat for Laurel. She had not had the opportunity or luxury before. Through all those years of school, she had been fortunate to keep up with her rent and groceries. Stillwater, Minnesota, was not at the top of her list of places she had planned to go, but right now it sounded good to her. Stillwater, such a symbolic name.

Her mother's letters had described the small picturesque town on the banks of the St. Croix River. It would be a white Christmas. This was the time to be with the people you cared for. She took a deep breath. She'd try not to think of Vittorio now; she wanted to anesthetize her memory.

Looking out of the window as the plane made its landing, she surveyed the icy scene below. Miniature snowplows were at work on the runways, and everywhere there was a white blanket of snow. In just a few short hours she had been transferred into a decidedly different environment.

They were funneled out of the aircraft directly into the airport complex. She saw her mother's anxious face, and Laurel fell into her arms, crying, laughing, hugging. Her stepfather, Walter, went for the luggage, and soon they were on their way.

Stillwater was all her mother had described. Dotted with church steeples, mantled by snow, the small city was almost a Currier and Ives painting come alive. Much of the town was being restored to what it once was in the late 1800s, recapturing the atmosphere of its river-lumber town origins, yet it was a thriving, active modern community as well. Her stepfather's work in an electronics firm was one of several such businesses nearby, and her mother felt very much at home in the friendly commmunity.

The river below was a surprise to her, frozen solid, covered in part by snow, its icy surface dotted here and there with what looked like small plywood huts and snowmobiles skimming to and fro. Even in the winter, it seemed, the river served as a recreation spot.

The house was brick, built on a slight slope, quite modern in appearance. The garage, on one side, opened directly into a large finished basement with two bedrooms, bath, and a family room. They climbed the stairs to the main level, and Laurel was ushered into a pleasant room with a four-poster bed and quilt that she recognized.

"You still have it!" She laughed and hugged the familiar patchwork to her cheek.

"Of course. Did you really think I would part with your first effort?" Her mother gave Laurel another hug and said, "You look so tired. You must be exhausted."

"I've been working pretty hard, Mom, and the anticipation of making this trip and all—it's probably all catching up with me."

"I'm cooking all your favorites for dinner. Rest up, if you'd like. We'll have plenty of time to talk. I do have some disappointing news. The boys have the flu in Vermont, so they aren't coming."

Laurel was disappointed because she had hoped to see her brother and his family. It had been so long since she'd seen them. "Guess that will give me a good reason to get to Vermont someday." She smiled. "I'm glad that at least I could make it."

"We are too." Her mother's voice was filled with emotion. "I must get to that dinner." She closed the door quietly behind her.

Laurel unpacked carefully and thought how unreal it seemed that she had left California just a few hours before and now she was in Minnesota, immersed in snow, in her mother's new home. She noticed in the car how well her mother looked. Certainly Minnesota and Walter must agree with her. It had been a long time since she'd seen her so radiant. Laurel looked in the mirror at her own wan face, a sharp contrast, she thought, to her mother's.

Dinner was all that was promised, including custard for dessert, a childhood treat. Walter appeared delighted with Laurel's presence. He had a gentle way of teasing her mother. "Do you think you cooked enough, Nell? Looks as if you were expecting four daughters."

"Never you mind. We don't seem to have too much trouble with leftovers around here," she chided, glancing at Walter's ample frame.

"We've saved the tree trimming for you, Laurel," he said. "Of course, we thought you were going to have some help from the boys, but I'm sure we'll manage. Your mother and I haven't put up such a big tree for a couple of years, just seemed too much trouble."

Each ornament was a memory of Christmases past, a trip in nostalgia—ceramic ornaments made in grade school, felt and glitter creations. Laurel gave her mother the stained-glass angel purchased at the art fair.

"Beautiful!" she exclaimed and quickly placed it on the tree. "Tomorrow is Christmas Eve, and now I feel ready."

With the room lights off, they sat there in the darkness, surveying their handiwork. Laurel's thoughts turned to her father and their many Christmases together. It was all right now. She missed him, but she knew he would be glad that her mother had found new happiness. He had been a loving man, and Laurel was content with it, truly at peace with his absence for the first time. Looking at the tree, she sighed, "It's lovely."

"Get to bed, young lady," her mother ordered.

Laurel felt comforted in her mother's "mothering" and gave her a light kiss.

Walter hugged Laurel. "Tomorrow we'll go ice fishing, if you'd like."

"I want to experience all Minnesota has to offer," Laurel agreed.

"Sitting on top of an ice slab all day, looking in a hole, isn't my idea of a good time," her mother commented.

"Now, Nell, you wouldn't pass up a giant northern pike, would you?"

"I'll believe that when I see it," she joked. "There's a lot of fishing done in this house without too much evidence of it."

"She's a hard woman, Laurel, but tomorrow we'll prove her wrong."

Soon Laurel was curled under the familiar quilt, thankful that exhaustion numbed the barbed thoughts of Vittorio that festered in her mind.

She was a bit apprehensive but game for her first ice-fishing experience. Walter had the snowmobile off the trailer, ready with the dog sled's metal frame loaded to capacity, hooked up to the snow bike. At least that's what she thought they resembled.

"We've had an early winter and don't have to worry about thin ice, but I'll be going pretty fast, just in case. Out where my shanty is, the river's slow and the ice is about six feet thick or more. Put on the helmet and hang on."

The sensation of moving fast over the snow-covered ice was exhilarating, the cold biting at her nose even through her mask. *Vittorio would love this*, she thought, and for a moment a deep sorrow enveloped her.

They stopped beside a small plywood box-like house, and she heard her feet crunch the snow as she helped Walter unload the sled of its contents—a bucket of minnows, lunch, thermos, an auger, stove, diesel oil, and what looked like a strange fishing tackle.

Walter soon had the stove going inside the hut, and they sat on makeshift benches, warming themselves, drinking mugs of hot coffee. He took the auger, went out of the shelter and cut several holes about eight inches across through the ice. Laurel joined him and looked down into the inky environment. Nearby were several other similar huts. Their owners popped out and gave Walter a friendly wave.

"This is a tip-up." Walter took the wooden frame and set it over the hole, baited a nylon line with a minnow, and dropped it into the black, bottomless pit. "If we get a strike, this flag will get triggered."

Laurel helped him bait the other holes, and

then Walter said, "Now, we watch. Fishing is a good excuse to do a lot of sitting."

They returned to their small wood-framed refuge, welcoming its warmth.

"This is pretty cozy," Laurel remarked. "The lengths some people will go to for fishing!" She laughed. "My friends in California will have a hard time believing this."

"How are things in California? I hope you know that if you ever want a change, you're welcome to stay with us."

Laurel looked at the kindly man across from her. "Thank you, Walter, I'll remember that." She looked down at her coffee.

"It's just that I noticed you don't look quite yourself, and your mother and I have been worried."

Laurel concentrated on her coffee cup. Was it so obvious, her preoccupation with another problem? She had hoped that she had done a better job of concealing her feelings. Having it brought to her attention again brought that old, familiar tightness to the pit of her stomach.

"Laurel," Walter said gently, "I know you once had a difficult time accepting me, but I want you to know I'm your friend."

"I can't talk about it, Walter," she choked, and then added, "but I want you to know that I'm very happy that you and Mom found each other." She kept her head bowed.

"You know, Laurel, we were very frightened at first."

"Frightened?" Laurel looked up.

"Yes, we both had been doing our own thing for several years before we met. I was lonely, but the thought of loving again, trusting again, adapting to a shared life-style was a risk, and your mother was afraid too. Thank heaven, we did take the risk."

The tears were now running down her cheeks. Trust, risk—was that what she had refused to accept? Emidio had said it too.... "A blend is like a good marriage, bringing the best qualities of each to create something new." Trust, risk.... Maybe she had jumped to conclusions because she lacked courage.

Walter put his arms around her. "Whatever your problem, give it time," he soothed.

Laurel swallowed some coffee and glanced out the door. "The flag!" she screamed. "The flag!"

The other fishermen were shouting, "Flag's up—flag's up!" rushing to the hole.

Laurel peered down and saw only a black emptiness. Walter showed her how the line was being pulled, indicating that something was on the other end.

"It's your hole, Laurel," he said. "Pull him in"

She looked astonished, but everyone was encouraging her. "Use your hands like this," one of the men demonstrated. She shucked off one of her mittens and grabbed the line. Hand over hand, she felt the tension.

"Keep it steady," they cautioned. "Steady."

She certainly had something. To Laurel it felt as if she had a whale. Whatever it was, it was twisting the line, but she kept pulling up, trying to keep the line from catching on the edge of the hole.

Everyone watched in anticipation. The line slipped from her hands and jerked her toward the hole. She gained control again, her hands working in rhythm now, keeping the tension even. As the fish came into view, it turned, and Laurel momentarily felt like releasing this powerful, struggling live thing, but the expressions on the faces of the fishermen prodded her into continuing. The fish was a ferocious-looking beast.

"It's a northern," one of the men shouted.

"A beauty, almost a twenty-incher!"

Everyone congratulated her on her catch, but she was only too glad to turn it over to Walter. In some ways it was a hollow victory. The fish's will to survive had been so intense that Laurel felt sorry for her antagonist. Hardly the proper fishing spirit, but Walter was thrilled, and the fish would make some splendid meals.

The others extended their hands, saying, "Good catch," and she shook each hand offered her. Her hands were beginning to ache from the cold, and she looked for her mitten. Someone came up to her, held her hand firmly, and started to rub the circulation back. He was holding her mitten. Laurel looked up, and, even behind his face mask, she recognized him.

"Vittorio!" she gasped.

"None other."

"How did you—"

"I hope you don't mind."

"Mind?" she answered, rushing into his arms.

Walter came up to them. "Seems like you've caught yourself an even bigger fish," he said, laughing.

Once again in the shanty, Laurel introduced the two men. Sitting on the wooden bench, she had trouble assimilating that out in the middle of the ice-capped St. Croix, Vittorio was beside her, but she knew that, without reservation, she was glad.

Walter tactfully excused himself to check the other holes and visit one of his fisherman pals.

"Your mom sent me with these—" Vittorio pointed to a sack of sandwiches.

"You've met my mom?"

"How else did you think I would have found you out here? But actually, I warned her last night that I was coming and asked her not to tell you." He put his arms around her, and she felt warmed through.

"Forgive me," he whispered in her ear.

"Vittorio, it was my—"

"We can argue about that later." He smiled and kissed her. "Oh, Laurel, I love you so much!" She clung to him, and the tears over-flowed. "It's that bad?" He held her close.

"That good," she managed to choke out be-tween sobs.

Walter returned to the shanty, and the two men did justice to the lunch. All Laurel could do was pick at hers and hold Vittorio's hand so it wouldn't disappear.

They talked about the wine business, the electronic business, about Minnesota and ice fishing. Content just to lean against Vit-torio's shoulder, she listened to the sound of the two men's voices, warm once again, the winter storm, that had so recently sapped her of her energy, now vanquished.

She rode back behind Vittorio on the snow-mobile he had borrowed from a neighbor. Flying over the ice and snow, she pressed her face against him, relishing the feel of his strong back. All that mattered was that he was with her now.

CHAPTER TWELVE

A light snowfall, which had started back at the shanty, had increased in volume by the time they returned to the house. Rooftops, mud, and pavements were once again covered over by a white, shining majesty. Christmas Eve, this world would be unblemished. Laurel stood beside Vittorio on the deck that ran the length of the back of the house, celebrating in the beautiful sight.

Vittorio seemed to settle into the family as one of their own, clearing the dishes, joking with her mother, comfortable with Walter, as if their friendship went back much further than just a few hours.

Her mother had taken Laurel aside to explain. "Actually, Laurel, I didn't have much choice. He just said he was coming, and you looked so miserable. I didn't think it could make you feel any worse."

Vittorio had certainly been the proper antidote for Laurel's depression, and her mother and Walter didn't question the relationship, just seemed to accept that she and Vittorio were a pair, and they were happy for Laurel's obvious pleasure in his being there.

Walter came out on the porch. "Aren't you getting chilled out here?"

"Hadn't noticed," Vittorio joked. Shaking the snowflakes from their hair, they went in and sat by the tree. They sipped steaming mugs of grog, while Laurel surveyed the inviting gifts under the tree.

"The kids aren't here, so why don't we open our presents tonight?" Laurel suggested.

"She always asks that," her mother explained with a mock pained expression. "It's almost a tradition for her to ask and for me to refuse. Good night, you two. We're glad you could join us for Christmas, Vittorio."

As soon as they left the room, Vittorio took her in his arms. "Laurel, I've had too much time to think these past weeks, and I was—"

She put her fingers to his lips to silence him.

"No, let me speak," he insisted. "I realize how I must have sounded that afternoon at the cabin. I'm used to running things, and I had that afternoon so clearly planned in my mind. I knew how I felt about you, and because everything was settled in my mind— Well, I thought it was settled in yours, and when your mood changed so abruptly and you seemed to be running away from me—"

He hesitated again. "Well, darn it, I was afraid."

"Afraid!"

"Yes." He looked at her steadily. "Afraid of losing you."

"Oh, Vittorio." Laurel wanted to make him understand. She felt humble by his admission. "It wasn't your fault. You were right when you said I couldn't lead with my heart." She remembered her conversation with Walter. Safety wasn't enough. "I was afraid too."

"And now?"

"I'm learning," she said. "I'm learning because I love you. It's just that when I saw those darn macadamia nuts in the cupboard, I—"

"Macadamia nuts? Cupboard? Did I miss something?"

"At the cabin."

Vittorio rolled his eyes to the ceiling. "Pam always gives me tons of them, trying to make me a convert. I just took a couple of cans—"

"You don't have to explain. I was so foolish."

"Pam is just an old friend, Laurel, a lonely friend who needed my help, and now John seems to be helping her drop some of her pretenses."

Laurel pulled him toward her, running her hands through the sides of his hair, placing them behind his neck, gently massaging away the tension that she felt in the strong muscles there.

"It will take more than patience and understanding to control myself if you don't stop that. I love you, Laurel."

Reaching under the Christmas tree, he gave her a large square box. Her fingers fumbled with the ribbon. She peeked in, lifting the tissue and then covering the object again.

"Don't you like it?"

"I love him," and she lifted out a stuffed toy tiger, with a pink ribbon around its neck.

"It's a her—can't you tell?"

Tied to the ribbon was a plastic bag, inside of which was an envelope. Opening the envelope, a picture of Mooch fell out, and attached to the picture was another envelope. On the back of Mooch's picture was the inscription, *Mooch misses you and loves you, and so do I—V.* She opened up the smaller envelope and drew out a gorgeous diamond solitaire.

"You don't have to wear it yet. I'm not rushing you, but when you're ready, I want you to have it and to put it on."

"Put it on me now, Vittorio."

"Are you sure?"

"Yes," she said seriously. "I love you."

He placed it on her left ring finger, the lights from the tree reflecting in the large stone.

"It's my mother's diamond, in a new setting."

"That makes it even more special." She admired the ring on her hand. "But it's a little loose."

"I thought I had your fingers memorized, but it proves once again I'm not infallible."

"Nice to hear you admit it," she teased.

"We can have it sized as soon as we get back." He held her hand. "To think I almost lost you! I've been going crazy these past few weeks. Then when you left, I knew I had to follow."

"I'm so glad you did." She nestled against him. "I was so miserable. Coming here in this setting with Walter and Mom helped me to realize that to love is to trust."

Vittorio was nuzzling her hair, his lips close to her ear. "I can't stand being parted from you."

Palpitations, call it whatever, Laurel knew that if he didn't stop nibbling her ear, she might lose any semblance of propriety she possessed. She stood up, and he held her in an embrace that made her breath come in short gasps.

"I love you," she said and closed her bedroom door, leaving him to go to his.

The snow had stopped falling now, and the full moon illuminated her room, reflecting off the stunning white woodland. Nothing could be this perfect, stay this perfect. She shook off the feeling of apprehension. *Accept it, Laurel. Don't fight it. Enjoy, enjoy.* She climbed into her bed and imagined what it would be like to sleep next to Vittorio in the cabin's giant feather bed. That's where she wanted to spend the first night of her marriage. She looked at the diamond, at the stuffed tiger guarding her bed. This was reality, not just a dream.

Her mother and Walter's response was predictable—excited and pleased. "I don't know which of yesterday's catch your mother was more surprised at, Vittorio or the northern pike," Walter said.

"That's easy," her mother responded, "the pike."

Opening the Christmas presents, preparations for dinner, poring over family albums, and stories of her childhood as related by her mother to Vittorio, took up most of the day. Vittorio explained that he must leave the next morning because he had left the winery at a difficult time.

Logically Laurel understood his reasons for leaving—the fire and its consequences and his business with the Calomenis. It was decided that she would stay on a few days, so her visit would not be too abrupt, but at the moment of parting all those reasons seemed insufficient.

On the way to the airport she kept the conversation light. "I want to spend my honeymoon at the cabin."

He looked surprised.

"What I mean is, I want to sleep in it the first night of our marriage."

"In what?" Vittorio grinned suggestively.

"In the bed, you idiot, that feather bed."

"Laurel—" He was laughing now. "Laurel, Laurel, no wonder I love you."

They hugged each other tightly, and she held to her promise not to shed any tears until she saw his plane lift off the runway. Biting her lower lip, she returned to Stillwater.

Walter and her mom were anxious to know the details of her relationship with Vittorio, and she tried to explain some of what had transpired, omitting, of course, the private details, but explaining her reluctance to marry such a strong, decisive personality.

"You're strong, too, in your own way, Laurel," her mother commented.

"Yes, I am." Saying it aloud was an affirmation. "I am."

"You bring him your strength, your love."

At the moment, it was sufficient to be loved by Vittorio and to love him in return.

The past months certainly had not been what Laurel had expected when she went to work at the winery, not what she imagined she'd wanted at the time—escape and solitude. Thank heaven, she thought, an alternative without Vittorio seemed almost impossible to her now.

On Thursday, parting from her mother and Walter was not as difficult as she imagined it would be, because she knew they would all be reunited for the wedding. She promised to let them know as soon as the date was set. Secured once again in the jet, she remembered how just a few days ago she had wondered where her destiny lay. Now the question was answered. She was to be Vittorio's partner in life.

Arriving in San Francisco, she scanned the airport lounge for him and saw Tony instead. "Vittorio asked me to pick you up—he couldn't get away. Don't look so disappointed. But I do see you look a lot better than when I put you on the plane. Tell me what happened in Minnesota."

"What did Vittorio tell you?" she asked.

"Not much, but he came back looking pretty smug himself."

Evidently Vittorio hadn't mentioned the engagement, so she decided to keep mum until she talked to him. She wasn't wearing the ring because it was loose. Not wanting to lose it, the diamond was concealed on a chain around her neck. "No news is good news," she quipped.

"A lot has happened around here since you've been gone." Tony filled her in. "The winery is back in working order. Any traces of smoke have been washed down the drain, and the wines are safe, much to Emidio's relief. Orders for the Heritage wine have been unprecedented, and fortunately we have enough to fill them. It's something about the name. The wine's excellent, but I think the public isn't always that discerning. The name had helped to make it popular."

Laurel smiled at Tony's assumption. Even a name couldn't make a bad wine good, but he had a point. Certainly "Heritage" appealed to tradition, good taste, and nostaligia. It was well named.

"Also, I settled my move to San Francisco with Vittorio, and he took it well. Right now he's in negotiations with the Calomenis."

"Any trouble?"

"No, not yet." Tony looked concerned.

"Remember what I said about borrowing trouble," she said.

After unpacking her suitcase, Laurel headed straight for Emidio's. It was twilight, the sun just an ember on the horizon. When she went up the steps, she heard Mooch bark a greeting. He leaped up, licked her face, and then tore through the house, jumping on chairs, running round and round, as if he couldn't contain his joy at seeing her again.

"This is my most enthusiastic welcome. I hope he wasn't too much trouble."

"No, just good company," Emidio patted Mooch, who seemed delighted with all the attention and thumped his tail on the floor.

"You're looking much better," Emidio said.

"I'm feeling much better." She gave him a quick hug. "But I can't stay and visit now."

Laurel was bursting to tell him the news and thought she might if she stayed any longer. Mooch jumped into the car, indicating he was aware of the transfer of ownership.

Vittorio was waiting on the porch steps, with his head in his hands, looking tired and drawn, when she returned.

"I'm sorry I couldn't meet you at the airport."

She gave him a perfunctory kiss. "I was too."

"Want to go out to dinner?" The invitation sounded halfhearted.

"How about soup and a sandwich?" she offered.

"I knew there was a good reason I wanted to marry you." He came up behind her and put his arms around her. "You can read my mind."

She twisted away, "And I'm not sure it's on food."

"Where's your ring?"

"Around my neck until we get it sized."

"Thought for a minute you might have changed your mind."

"No such luck," she bantered.

He scooped her up into his arms. Just his touch sent ripples of pleasure through her. "I've had a long trip, and I need a shower," she said.

"I'll help you," he teased.

"No need." Laurel handed him a magazine. "Afterward we should talk," she said.

"Agreed," he said. "About what?"

"About our engagement announcement for one thing."

"I've alerted Angie to a possible dinner party Sunday evening. How's that sound?"

"Sounds wonderful."

"Now that's settled." He came closer.

She held her hand up in a stop motion. "I can't think when you—"

"That's the idea."

"Oh, yes." She remembered what she wanted to ask him. "How are things going with the negotiations?"

His face took on a closed look. "I don't want to talk about it, Laurel. I'm being outbid, and that's all I'm going to say."

"What are you going to do?" she probed.

"That's business."

"But I love you and want to help."

"The only way you can help me now is to remain silent." He looked at her sternly, reminding her of the time he thought she was trespassing on his property.

Her voice rose. "You're shutting me out."

"Even in a marriage, some decisions must ultimately be made alone," he said.

"Talking something over doesn't rob a person of his decisions," she said, irritated. "Vittorio, maybe I can help you with—"

"I said I didn't want to discuss it." His voice was firm.

Without a word Laurel turned her back on him and went to the stove, opened a can of

tomato soup, and made a couple of sandwiches. Neither of them ate.

After a few minutes of silence Vittorio got
up and headed for the door. "I have to get up
early in the morning." He hesitated.

She fingered the diamond around her neck.
He gave her a soft kiss, holding her just a
moment before leaving.

Laurel was left with two bowls of tomato
soup, which she poured down the sink. She
gave Mooch the sandwiches and sat in her
rocker, wondering how she was going to live
with a man who, when he wanted to avoid a
subject, just refused to talk to her.

It was evident that something must be
wrong. She could sense it. Was he so intent
on having the property that he would go to
any lengths to get it? Have Sam keep his
promise, sell to Vittorio for less than offered
by others, create a rift between John and his
father, Julie and her brother, make Tony
take sides? Sides, consequences—Laurel felt
frustrated.

"Vittorio always gets what he wants," was
what Tony had said, but at any cost? Perhaps
Tony's fears were groundless, but this was all
speculation on her part, because Vittorio refused to discuss it with her.

She twisted the chain around her neck and
stared at the ring. Something was wrong,
and Vittorio was hiding it from her. She
loved him. "Darn it—I won't let you hide!"

she shouted to the empty room. Mooch wagged his tail in agreement.

Vittorio wasn't at the winery on Friday. Laurel touched the ring around her neck, a symbol of their commitment, a pledge. There was a gulf between them now that needed to be bridged, a wall that separated them as surely as if it were made of stone. They would have it out before they announced their engagement on Sunday. Tomorrow was Saturday, and she wouldn't allow Vittorio to avoid her.

The next morning Vittorio was gone. She heard his Ferrari come up the drive in the early afternoon, and he walked up to the top of the property. An hour went by, and he hadn't returned. She became concerned. Jogging up the road, she found him sitting on an old stump, staring at the vineyards. She approached him quietly.

"I'm glad you came," he told her.

"Am I supposed to be a mind reader, to know when it's all right to intrude and when it's not?"

"That would be a nice quality to have." He tucked her hand under his arm. "I don't mean to be so hardheaded. I wanted to talk to you about it, but my pride gets in the way sometimes. I had to think it through."

"I wouldn't have let it stay in the way too long." She nudged him in the ribs.

"I know that too," he said. "When I first

met you, I was attracted to you. I will admit, darling, your physical attributes impressed me first, and they still send me in a tailspin. But once I knew you, I realized what substance you had. I need you, Laurel. I need your gentle way, your kind of honesty, your kind of wisdom, even when I seem least receptive.

"I lost the Calomeni deal," he confided.

"How?"

"I released Sam from his promise."

"I think you made the right decision, Vittorio," she whispered.

"It just wasn't worth the cost of dividing the family."

"I know what it cost you," she answered.

"Only one dream," he said. "I'll find another way."

The bridge was crossed, the wall removed. They talked a long time, watched the sun go down on the now stripped and pruned vines. It was like their relationship, stripped and pruned of unnecessary subterfuge, more honest now, and yet with space for growth.

Together they started down the drive, and then Vittorio stopped, laughing his deep, comforting laugh.

"Whatever are you laughing at?"

He just stood there, his shoulders shaking until the tears ran down his cheeks.

"Are you going to let me in on the joke? Is it about the winery?"

"The winery? No, something much more important than that, my little tiger. Just feathers." He whirled her around. "Just hundreds and thousands and millions of feathers!"